The Gentle Art of Making Enemies

Volume II

ISBN: 0615879780

ISBN-13: 978-0615879789 (paledark Books)

Kevin Mellor

The Gentle Art of

Making Enemies:

Volume II

by

Kevin Mellor

Kevin Mellor

43

<u>Dave</u>

Let me go on record as saying that I never thought it was a good idea for that chick to hook up with us. I don't hate her guts or anything. I haven't formed an opinion of her, good or bad. She's not bad looking, except for her ass, which looks kind of weird, and I'm willing to chalk that up to the fact that she wears pants that are kind of baggy, but whatever. It's all about logic, me and her. I'm a guy, and all my parts work. I don't have trouble getting a boner or anything, and I'm not into guys. So she's kind of attractive to look at, and I'm a guy with a working boner and two feelings--horny and more horny--so hell yeah, I wanna harass her with my wiener. But I'm a guy and she's a chick, and therefore she's a pain in the ass. I'm not saying she means to be. I'm not saying she wants to be. I'm just saying she *is*.

After Pete got bitch-whapped, we should have left it at two. It's like we're the Jon Spencer Blues Explosion--I'm Jon Spencer, Lucas is Judah Bauer, Pete was Russell Simins. Everybody has a role, everybody contributes to the whole. If Russell Simins died in a boating accident, you don't just go out and get another fucking drummer and say "Yeah, hey, look at us, we're still the Jon Spencer Blues Explosion." Fuck that shit. Granted, I'm still awesome, because I'm Jon Spencer. Lucas is still Judah Bauer, the man with the axe in his hand and a fucked up way of playing the blues. If you still wanna rock, you get a drum machine. You don't go get the fucking drummer from Luscious Jackson and call it the

Blues Explosion. That's a rip-off. You can still go see them play, and it'll be a kick ass show, but it's not gonna be like the old days.

Common sense dictates that if you get hauled in by the cops because they suspect you of something you actually did, and then you get lucky and they let you go, you quit while you're ahead. And if you don't want to quit altogether, then you at least lay off for a while. In our case, we should have packed up and left town first chance we got. I was ready to go. It's not like college is enjoyable or fulfilling in any way. Not to mention that winter was coming on in a few weeks or so, and I think cold and snow are absolute bullshit.

But we didn't go. One of us was still worried about classes and rent they'd already paid. One of us was being a big bloody fucking albatross around the neck of the other two. And if you're still not catching on, I'll tell you-- it wasn't Lucas.

She kept whining about some soratory bitches who had given her a mean look or wouldn't lend her a tampon when she needed it or something. She tried Lucas, and he wouldn't bite. Then she tried me, and I told her it wasn't my call. In hindsight, this was not the best strategic move I could have made. She left me alone, which was all I really wanted at the time, but instead of just dropping it like a civilized person, she kept after Lucas about it. Nevermind that we were officially under suspicion, or that there were suddenly people we didn't know parked down the street who didn't seem to do anything but sit in their cars, read the paper and drink coffee. She had a serious hard-on for those bitches, and she wasn't going to let it go.

This is not to say that she wore Lucas down against his will or better judgment. Neither one of those things is possible, as far as I can tell. What it did was make him think. And Lucas, thinking, is not something to fuck around with. He started watching the cops who were watching us. We started taking nice little walks to figure out just where and how they could follow us.

It only took him about four days to figure a way around them. The two of us went to the library one night with a change of clothes in our backpacks, through the front door, took the stairs up to the top floor, looked up some old issues of *Rolling Stone* just to kill some time, and then took the rear stairs down to the basement. Lucas slapped some duct tape on the self-locking door beside the loading dock to keep it from latching. We cut across the south quad, past the football stadium, and straight over to that chick's apartment. Nothing to it.

So blah blah, Tits got her way. We changed clothes and went out the back door of her place, to the soratory chick apartment a few doors down from hers. Getting in was easy. Her Highness just knocked on the door, and when they looked through the little curtain and saw it was her, they opened right up.

It was a boring beginning. Things didn't improve.

I'd found a plunger and was stamping bloody circles on the group pictures on the walls, because I find art in any medium and form to be nothing less than fascinating, and we were pretty much just standing around anyway.

"It's odd that they would actually have a plunger," I said, and pulled it off the wall with a disgusting popping sound.

"Why?" she said.

"I don't know. I guess I just never took into consideration that maybe soratory chicks took big dirty craps that clogged the toilet. What with them being bulimic whores and all I figured they threw up too much to have anything left to crap out."

"I don't think they're all bulimic," she said.

"Oh sure," I nodded. "Some of them are probably anorexic."

"So you think having some sort of eating disorder is a requirement for being a member of a sorority?"

The thing about that chick, and I'm not saying it's a bad thing, is that anytime she begins a sentence with the word "So," you know she's looking to talk some shit. It's like trying to sneak up on somebody while you're giggling.

"What else could it be?" I said.

"Too much money? Being so insecure you have to pay for your friends? A latent love of date rape?"

Not the most original explanations, but coming from a chick, they were definitely funny to me in a different light. Of course, you'll have to remember that I was the most bored I'd ever been while playing with human blood, so you know, any port in a storm.

"Well, sure," I said. "But if you eat something and then let your body digest it, they probably throw you out even if you are really stupid and shallow in every possible way."

"Why?"

I flung the plunger across the room to see what kind of sound it would make. Low thump when the rubber hit the wall, sharp pop right after when the handle made contact, muted thud on the carpet. "Maybe those ass paddles make a better popping sound if they're hitting bone instead of meat," I told her.

Lucas was in his cobra mode, not really paying attention to either of us. The awesome thing about the cobra mode is, I'm 100% sure he doesn't do it on purpose. He stands almost perfectly still, watching them, waiting for them to do anything so he can strike at them again, and he only blinks about once every two minutes. I doubt he even knows he does it.

She watched him do this for a couple of seconds and I could tell she didn't understand it. It's one of those things you pick up on after a while. "Did you ever notice that you can't win an argument with him, even by pointing out the obvious flaws in his logic?" she said.

Lucas flicked ashes on the carpet and didn't move his head. "It's one of his more endearing qualities."

"You should see the other one," I told her.

"The ability to eat until your stomach bursts?" she said.

"I think that's more amazing than endearing."

"You know what's amazing to me? That I keep talking to you."

"Not as amazing as the fact that you've known me for almost six weeks and haven't slapped me or put out yet. You're not even really a chick, are you? Level with me. You started dressing like a girl so you didn't have to do anything but walk laps in gym class, didn't you?" I grinned. "Come on, I'm hip. I bet you're hung like a bull alligator."

She had a confused frowny-smile. "A bull alligator?"

"Don't change the subject."

There were only two of the sluts left--*Dawn* and *Heather*--tied to kitchen chairs and boo-hooing behind the duct tape we'd put over their mouths. I hate that. I don't want to know their fucking names. But after we'd gotten in there our slut just *had* to tell us, like it made any fucking difference. I don't know what they'd done to her, and I didn't care. They were kind of hot; if we'd gone in there like usual, with Lucas pointing the way and none of us knowing anything about them, it probably would have been a good time. But no, she had to tell us their names.

I was not having a good time.

In fact, I was pretty fucking pissed off.

The other two--*Laura* and *Teri*--were already done, laying on the couch with their guts ripped open and splashed all over the place. What a fucking joke. But I did learn that you can do a few interesting things with a toilet plunger and a gaping hole in a stomach, so the night hadn't been a total loss.

"This doesn't seem right," I said. I was so pissed off I was getting a headache. "It's way too easy."

"Easy like how?" Rachel said.

"They're all tied up like pigs. Where's the fun in that?"

She shrugged. "What do you usually do with them?"

"Usually they're all running around in nighties or half-naked or something and we get to chase them around," I said. "It's pretty exciting. And if you have trouble catching one and you get mad about it, it's really fun to just stab the fuck out of her for making you look stupid." I looked at Lucas. "We should cut them loose."

He nodded at me and didn't say anything. I could tell his heart wasn't in it either.

The chair chicks started really crying it up when Rachel took her knife and cut the ropes around the first one's feet. She had nice feet, tangerine polish on her toenails, just a little bit of blood drying on the tops from where it had splashed on her. Nice job on shaving her legs, too. They weren't bumpy or anything. It made you wonder how far up the shave-job went, and if it kept the same quality when you got there. I like it when a girl is completely bald from the waist down on both sides.

And that was all it took. My headache had switched heads, if you know what I mean, and I liked the new one.

"You think they've got any condoms laying around here?" I said to no one in particular.

Rachel's head snapped around. "Oh my God. Are you really going to--"

"What are you, insane?" I said, realizing for the first time that I had made Olympic circles on the wall with the bloody plunger and wondering what, if anything, that might mean about my subconscious. "Of course I am. These chicks are fucking hot."

44

<u>Rachel</u>

The next day, cops and reporters and gorehounds were so thick outside my apartment complex that I had to camp out at the house. It seems obvious, in hindsight, that you shouldn't shit where you eat, but I wasn't thinking that far in advance at the time. Everything was more along the lines of *"We can kill people I hate and get away with it? What are we waiting for?"*

Looking back on it, I was a real ass about the whole thing. Those two guys had enough to think about without me dumping more on top of it, but it was like I couldn't help myself. And if we're going to be honest about it, I guess I didn't try very hard. Childish and petty as it was, I wanted to see Lucas make a grand gesture on my behalf. I knew Dave would go along with it, even if he didn't want to, and that wasn't without an appeal of its own.

Lucas is not the boss, at least not in a traditional sense. He tells you something, or says that you should do something, and you do it, because you trust him for whatever reason. At first I didn't like it. If you're going to trust someone it only makes sense that you know why. I still don't.

He takes you under his wing. You watch him and see how he reacts or doesn't react, or filter through the sarcasm and oddity of whatever he says. When he actually says anything at all it's usually in reply to someone else. He's not prone to starting conversations or even participating in them unless he needs to or the urge strikes him. Ask him a question and he might answer it if you're lucky.

None of this is making him sound reliable or trustworthy, I know. He inspires a gut reaction. You look at him, and you just *know*. He's solely dedicated to his own preservation. He trusts no one. I believe that I'm his friend, to the extent that a person like Lucas can have a friend, and in the scope of what friendship means to him. He's helped Dave and I, several times, in all kinds of ways, but I believe that if either of us ever crossed him--not if we disagreed with him, but really, truly *crossed* him--he would kill us.

I know how terrible that sounds. I do. And I don't think anyone could ever understand how comforting it is to me in spite of that.

I slept in Peter's room. Lucas had moved into it, but he didn't seem to have much use for the bed. The sheets and blankets had an odor--Peter's, I assume. It wasn't bad, like a stink or anything. It just smelled like somebody's body. The idea of sleeping in a dead guy's bed, with the scent of him still lingering in it, was more than a little unsettling. Lucas was in the habit of working at his typewriter all night long, and the chatter of it was soothing, sort of like when you put a wind-up clock in with a litter of puppies. Whatever he was writing, there was a lot of it. Half a ream of paper was piled up on the desk beside the typewriter; every time he pulled a sheet out of the roller, he dropped it on the pile. And it wasn't like he'd type a sentence and then stop and think about whatever he was going to type next. Sometimes he'd do three or four pages and only stop to change sheets.

We all woke up late in the afternoon and puttered around the house, not really doing anything. Dave played the guitar and watched *The Jeffersons* marathon on *TV Land*, which made him laugh more than I thought it would. I always liked that show, so we bantered back and forth about what was going on in the episodes for a while. Lucas came in with a six-pack of Corona, a hot-water bottle, and a book and sat in the baby-blue horseshoe chair. He put the hot water bottle on his right side and started reading.

"What's with that?" I asked Dave, because if you know Lucas, that makes sense.

He shrugged. "He does that sometimes."

"What's wrong with you?" I said, this time to Lucas himself.

He didn't look up.

"Yeah, I like hot water bags too," I said, and Dave laughed. "Come on, tell me. If you tell me I'll be your girlfriend."

"No thanks."

"What do you mean, *'nuh thanks?'*" I said, and Dave shot me a look of wincing horror. I thought it was a pretty good impression of Lucas, considering the female vocal cords I have to work with. "You know you want me. I'm hot."

"Oh you're hot," Lucas said. He was looking at me then. Definitely not the way I'd wanted him to. "Nothing hotter than some bitch who got knocked up by a fucking frat rat."

That would have been a slap in the face from anybody. Coming from him, it made me feel about two inches tall. *"Knocked up by uh fuckin' frat rat,"* I mimicked. This time I leaned on the dumb accent of it hard, and Dave gigged me in the ribs with his elbow.

"Don't," he said under his breath.

I had Lucas' full attention then. You do not want Lucas' full attention. Ever. Very serpentine. Think of cobras with flared hoods, rattlesnakes coiled and shaking their maracas, pythons licking the air. No eyelids, roiling muscle. Venom and fangs.

"Hey," Dave said. "We should go to the store and get food. I've got money."

I saw what he was trying to do. I could have kissed him for it. On the cheek, anyway. If he'd shaved.

"Where'd you get money?" I said. "I want some."

"My parents sent me a check for the rent," Dave said. "Almost proving that they do serve some legitimate and useful function in the universe besides giving me something to mock and resent."

Lucas was still staring at me.

Dave gently laid his guitar down on the couch and wove the pick into the strings, over the neck. "Yeah, let's go to that grocery store place and buy some food-type crap. I'm hungry."

I flopped back comfortably just to show them that I was in no hurry and not the least bit intimidated, which was a total, screaming lie. "How are we going to get there?" I said. "Walk?"

"You are," Dave told me. "I'm going to ride you piggyback, because you're pregnant and need the exercise."

"You're always so thoughtful."

"Hey, just because you're a knocked-up slut doesn't mean you don't deserve some consideration," Dave said. "Some people would be all like 'Fuck that slutty cunt whore bitch and her fucking *Weekly World News* dog-baby,' but I was raised better than that."

"Jesus Christ!" I cried.

"No, he's dead," Dave said. "And I'm not ashamed to masturbate. Although we do both hang out with whores and lepers and look good with our arms stretched out. And our dads both give us shitty jobs to do all the time."

Uncomfortable silence.

"Alright then," I said. My palms were starting to sweat and I really needed to pee. "Let's go, if we're going."

After a quick trip to the little girls' room, we were on our way. As soon as we got outside and the door was shut behind us, Dave started laughing. "You should never, ever, *ever* do that again," he said. "Ever. Never-*ever*-never."

"What is it that I did, exactly?"

"Imitate him," he told me. "Pete did that once, in that dumb hick voice."

"What happened?"

"Lucas duct taped him to a chair and was going to gouge his eyes out with a corkscrew," he said, "but I talked him out of it."

"You're a nice guy."

"I know, it sucks sometimes," Dave sighed. He lit a menthol cigarette he'd scavenged up somewhere and spit a stray piece of tobacco off of his tongue. "I really wanted to see what that would have looked like, you know?"

45

Dave

I don't like the news even when I'm on it. Part of this, I'm sure, comes from the fact that I'm an egotistical, self-absorbed prick who doesn't really give a fuck what happens to people I don't know, especially if it's boring. The *WGN 9:00 News* in Chicago is usually okay, because there's always a lot of stabbings and beatings and fires and wrecks and little kids getting kidnapped or being found in an apartment with no heat being fed dog food by their mothers who are out sucking cock for crack, or something. These are not good things. I am not glad they happen. They are, however, interesting.

The news we got in Friedman was a fucking joke, seriously. If it wasn't for us and our hobbies, they wouldn't have had jack squat to talk about. Friedman doesn't even have TV news--they get it from Quincy, Illinois, and Hannibal, Missouri, those two great cultural centers of the mid-Midwest. Basically what you got was a lot of smiling good cheer about Dogwood Festivals, air shows, county fairs, blood drives, and whether or not the city council in Bladderville, Illinois was likely to approve a new tax referendum that would provide more money to keep the public pool open for the summer. Exciting stuff. Sometimes they'd have something about some white trash guys with tattoos and no shirts getting busted for making meth, or somebody being killed in a car accident or something, but mostly it was just a lot of feel-good crap that generally made you wish people were more inclined to do harm to each other on a regular basis for your own entertainment.

On the other hand, we were always the first thing they talked about, which was not only convenient for us, but did a fair job of stroking my fragile male ego. The news guy was a fucking tool who looked like the coach on *The White Shadow*, but he was talking about me, so I was willing to let it slide. He was standing outside Rachel's apartment complex looking like he was about to blow a wad in his pants. Totally repulsive. You could see the wheels spinning in his head, I'm not even kidding. This guy was already thinking about how long it would be until Tom Brokaw retired and he could slip into the chair, and you could read it all over his face. And he had the whole Geraldo Rivera phony-as-all-fuck thing going for him, which wasn't doing anybody any good.

"In spite of additional police patrols and local citizens' groups forming their own neighborhood watches, officials are still stumped as to who the killer--*or killers*--are. Peter Bilotti, the 22 year-old man found dead at a previous crime scene just two weeks ago, was believed to have been the killer. In light of these new murders, it seems that this accusation may have been premature. According to Lt. Rhodes, the officer heading the investigation, the possibility that Bilotti may not have been working alone has not been ruled out."

Woo-hoo, cut to tape. Lt. Rhodes, our fearless law enforcement leader, was sitting behind a desk wearing a short-sleeved white dress shirt and a striped tie, which is still the height of fashion among people who want to appear sophisticated and comfortable at the same time, then fail miserably at both. You kind of had to feel bad for the guy, though. He looked like someone had been giving him daily enemas with battery acid for at least a month.

"We still have reason to believe that Bilotti was present at at least one other crime scene, although we won't know that for sure until all the forensic evidence has been examined thoroughly. At this time we are not ruling out the possibility that the killer, whoever he may be, is not working alone. We are currently following several substantial leads in our search for who, if they exist, these other killers might be."

"That was informative," I said. "I particularly enjoyed the fluid use of the double *at*. Not many people can pull that off without looking like a complete idiot."

"Not much of a cop, but I think I'd buy a used car from him," Rachel said.

Now it was what Byrne had been waiting for--his turn to talk again. "Do you have any evidence that links these recent killings to the previous ones? Or is there a possibility that they may in fact be copycat killings?"

"Well, of course we're looking into that, but again, we won't be able to make a definite decision until the forensic team has gathered all the evidence and we've had a chance to examine it thoroughly," Rhodes said.

"*And thank you for your support,*" Rachel said, which I thought was pretty funny.

Cut the tape, back to Todd Byrne, boy reporter, in front of Rachel's building: "In related news, Cindy Dawson, sister of victim Katherine Dawson, held an emergency meeting last night to address citizens' concerns."

The question that immediately came to my mind after hearing this was, who the fuck is this bitch to be calling an "emergency" meeting for anything? Oh my God, the citizens are concerned! Call a meeting, before they riot!

But before we continue with this fond reminiscing, I would like to pause here for just a moment to talk about the concept of "normal" people and the medium of television.

My position is simple.

STAY THE FUCK OFF OF IT.

You're ugly. You stutter and stammer and blink too much. Your voice cracks at inopportune times, and anyone with a soul is pained to have to look at you while you try to put your best self forward for the sake of posterity and look like a horse's ass in the process.

Do you have any idea why celebrities look and sound good on television? They're all genetic freaks who hire other freaks, freaks who've spent the majority of their lives learning the fine arts of making a race of superhuman beings look like the most beautiful, desirable, together things in the universe as we know it. And when the hair-and-makeup freaks are done with our superhumans, more freaks are waiting in the wings. Freaks who know about things like lighting and wardrobe and camera angles. And this is the *Cliff's Notes* version of it, I swear. We're not even going to go into detail about the plastic surgeons, the diction coaches, the teeth-whitening dentists and posture tutors and fitness trainers and personal assistants. Behind every celebrity there is a Mongol horde of warriors, each with a specific duty and function, each working toward a common goal. For the most part I think that goal is to make you hate your pathetic, worker-bee life by making you so jealous of the luck and good fortune of others that you want to destroy them and then yourself, but that's neither here nor there.

What is here, because I say it is, is that we've been ingrained to unquestioningly hold different sets of standards when it comes to the attractiveness of celebrities and "normal" people. Those hot teenage chicks at the mall with the big hooters that you would sell your mom's rosary to ass-fuck? Put them on TV, and they're not hot at all. This is not to say that they're not attractive, and therefore not worthy of being rammed in the pooper, no way. They *are* cute, and you should go ahead and try to do all the brown-star astrology on them that you can, if you can talk them into it. Just don't think they're ever gonna look good on TV, cause it's not gonna happen.

Okay, anyway. So our hero, Cindy Dawson, is Oprah Winfrey-ing it up in front of a bunch of senior citizens in seed caps and bifocals and Sunday-go-to-meetin' clothes, as I've heard Lucas call them a couple of times. They're all sitting in folding chairs and blinking like constipated frogs when they realize that the camera may or may not be on them, all of them trying to look concerned, none of them trying to look too smart. Or at least I hope they weren't trying. Our hero, Cindy Dawson, is really attempting to rally the troops and provide material for a key scene in her future bio-pic, *Sisterly Justice*, or whatever the fuck they'll call it. Coming to *Lifetime*--television for women-- during sweeps week a couple years from now, or when we're all about to get executed.

Oh yeah, that crap about her being our hero? Calling that sarcasm is the equivalent of referring to the Titanic as "slightly damp."

I just thought I'd point that out.

"I know you're outraged at what's happening in this community, and you can well imagine how my family and the families of the other victims feel," the bitch was blathering. "But we need to remember two things--to be cautious, and that the police will catch this monster."

Pause for the applause of a few dozen soft, arthritic hands. A charming sound, not unlike me pissing into a container of sour cream in a quiet room.

"Who the hell *is* this bitch?" Rachel said.

"Nevermind that," I told her. "Where are they?"

"What?"

"Where'd they have this meeting?"

The three of us stared at the television, which of course chose that exact moment to put a nice shade of electric lime green over the picture. Fucking Zenith.

"It looks like one of those conference rooms they have in motels," Rachel said. She stood up and kicked the side of the TV, which made the green crap go away nicely.

"Which one?" I said. "There's at least four of them in this town."

"Five," Lucas said, because even though he's never stayed in any of them or known anyone who has, he carries that kind of information around with him.

"The Travel Inn," Rachel said.

"Man, I knew all that time you spent as a prostitute might come in handy," I told her, "but this is ridiculous."

She gave me a look so dirty it made my hair feel clean by comparison. "Look, jerk, when they show the old people again. It says so behind them, on the tablecloth."

Our hero, Cindy Dawson, was staring right at us. Through the crappy magic of television, boys and girls, she was looking right into our living room and into our *souls.*

Well, maybe not. But they did have a big close-up of her face. She wasn't bad looking, for an older chick. I kind of wanted to knock her teeth out with a hammer and rape her mouth until she choked on my come and her own saliva and blood, but the urge wasn't like, *overpowering* or anything. She probably only had a couple more good years left in her before the wrinkles started setting in and she got that weird fat on the back of her arms that chicks always end up with.

"And to the killer, if he's watching this, make no mistake about it," she said, really giving it all she had. "We *will* catch you. Your time is running out."

Those old people went off like somebody was giving away calendars and blood pressure medicine, and we could see it on the tablecloths behind them--The Travel Inn, stitched white and gold on royal blue.

"Holy shit, you're right," I said.

"I'm not as dumb as you look," Rachel said. "So what do you want to do about her?"

I stood up and raised my hand. "Could I have the floor?"

"The house recognizes the honorable senator from the

great state of Illinois," Lucas said, grinning out of one side of his mouth.

"I think we should go over there, sit down with her, and apologize from the depths of our cold, black hearts for all the suffering and misery we've caused her with our thoughtless, psychopathic actions," I said. "We'll get a pizza, cry for a while, and then handcuff ourselves to the bed with our kidneys facing the door, so the cops don't have to go through the trouble of positioning our bodies when they come in and beat the living shit out of us."

There was a moment of respectful contemplation. I may never go down in history as one of the all-time great orators, but I have my moments. Most of them when I'm masturbating, but why bring that into it?

"I don't know," Rachel said. "It seems like there's something missing in all that."

"Well," I shrugged, "we could find her room, wait for her to come outside, and cut her until she can't tell her intestines from her shoelaces."

"Yeah!" Rachel said.

"That's what I wanted to do all along, but that other plan sounded a lot classier, didn't it?"

"Oh definitely," she said.

46

Rachel

We were sitting in the Camaro in the back corner of the Travel Inn parking lot, doing absolutely nothing but watching Lucas smoke. Dave had been drinking cans of Red Bull one after another, which meant he was yakking at 110mph and about to fidget his way through the bottom of the car and wind up on the blacktop.

When Dave paused for breath, I said "Not to sound like a whiner or anything, but maybe we could have planned this out a little better."

"Yeah really," Dave said. "Why didn't we bring any pizza? Where the hell is the Mountain Dew? And how come you never bring any of your hot slutty friends over to do us?"

"I don't have any hot slutty friends."

"You're the only slut in the bunch, huh?" he said. "That's a bitch. I guess it cuts down on the competition, though."

"When we're done here, is it okay if I kill him next?" I asked.

"Do it outside the car," Lucas said, which surprised me, because I'd said similar things before and he'd never replied. "I don't think he left enough hamburger wrappers back there to soak up the mess."

Dave nodded and smiled, but didn't look too amused. "Not to be a whiny slut like Rachel, but I really have to piss. A lot."

"Tie a knot in it," I spat at him. The slut jokes were starting to get out of hand.

"Does your mom know you talk like that?"

"Taught me how," I said.

"Once again proving my theory that if you've had enough semen in your mouth it will eventually make you talk like a sailor."

Lucas flicked his cigarette butt into the parking lot and reached out the open window for the door handle. "I'm gonna go look around."

"By yourself?" Dave asked.

"No," Lucas said. Then he got out of the car and walked across the parking lot toward the back of the building. Alone.

Dave looked at me. "Inside that man's head is a strange, strange universe."

"The one in your head is never going to win any prizes either," I told him.

"Yeah, but at least mine has cable, except for *The Playboy Channel.*"

"I'm not even going to ask."

"I used to have that one too, but I broke my antennae trying to tune it in."

"How lovely for you," I said. "Seriously though, is there any chance at all of you just shutting the fuck up for a good hour or so? Just until the urge to puncture my eardrums with a sharpened #2 pencil subsides slightly?"

"Let me think about it," Dave said. He cupped his chin between his thumb and index finger and frowned for five seconds. "Nope, not gonna happen. Any chance of you giving me a fast, sloppy blowjob? Just a quick mouthfuck between friends?"

I flipped him off with both hands. "You talk a lot of shit, but I know better," I smirked. "If I said yes and leaned forward right now, you'd piss your pants. You'd bolt out of this car so fast we'd have to get a new door, because you'd take that one with you."

"You think?" Dave said. He was still smiling. Technically.

"Do you even *talk* to living girls?" I said. "Seriously. Like, when you're not about to gut them and rape their corpses with that child-like penis of yours?"

"I don't think it can technically be construed as 'rape' unless they complain about it, which they can't, because they're fucking dead," he said, and scratched at his sideburns. "You really think I'm hung like a little kid?"

"That's probably your hang-up right there," I told him, really beginning to enjoy myself. "You're worried about the size of your cock, like every other stupid guy."

"That doesn't matter?" he said.

"Sure it matters," I said. "What are you, stupid? Who the hell wants to get naked and spread their legs for somebody who's hung like your index finger? We could finger ourselves without some sweaty loser like you laying all over us."

Let's pause for a dose of reality here, shall we?

I've only had sex with three people, and they were all about the same size. Five or six inches and decent girth, I guess. Not porno cocks or anything. If I was Goldilocks, you could say I screwed three different Baby Bears, because they were all just right. Not too big, not too small. I tell you this not to sound like a whore--although I'm starting to, even to myself--but to let you know that all of that was for Dave's benefit, and that I am not some nasty size-queen skank.

Let me pause again to say that I'm really uncomfortable

with the direction this whole thing has started to take.

Anyway, Dave.

"See, your whole little argument, or whatever you want to call it, is a crock of horseshit," he said. "Because unless you drilled a peephole in the bathroom wall at our house, I'm fairly certain that you've never seen my penis, and that you're only calling it child-like because you're trying, in your cute, pathetic, laughable little way to get under my skin."

"I saw it last time," I lied. "In those few inept, fumbling seconds between the time it cleared your zipper and when you managed to start humping that nasty sorority slut."

"And you're prepared to call it child-like after a brief glimpse in the heat of a moment?"

"It doesn't matter how long I look at it, it's not going to get any bigger," I smiled. "Plus, the moment was not 'hot' in any sense of the word. Actually, that was one of the most disgusting things I've ever seen in my life, and I'm not *even* kidding."

He lit one of the cigarettes from the pack he'd bought with his rent check and offered me one. I declined. "What's this, silence?" I said. "You're not even going to attempt to defend yourself? Not one feeble excuse to be offered up?"

"Excuse for what?"

"Why you only date the dead," I said.

"Oh." He smoked and looked out the window. "What do you want to know?"

Now this was something I hadn't thought about. Seeing someone have sex with a corpse is a mind-numbing experience. When you see it there's only one thought in your head, very loud, and it sounds something like *oooh-jesus-fucking-disgusting*. It's more along the lines of something you block out than something you try to come up with questions about.

I stretched to one side to relieve the threat of a cramp in my left leg. "What can you possibly get out of it?" I asked. "How could that be any fun at all?"

"It's perfect," he shrugged.

"What do you mean, perfect?" I said. "They're *dead*. As in *not living*. How can that be perfect?"

He was quiet for a little bit, and I thought I'd finally stumped him. Then I leaned back slightly and realized he was laughing into the butt of his Marlboro Light.

"What's so funny?"

"Do you really think that you squirming around and moaning adds anything special to sex?" he said. "Your *personality*? That's hilarious. Don't take this personally, because I'm not talking about you in particular. I kind of like you, most of the time. But a girl isn't much more than a walking advertisement for sex and a maintenance system for a cunt."

"Jesus Christ!" I cried. "You really think that?"

"That's what I'm talking about," he grinned, and shot at me with his index finger. "You all think you're so special, that the whole world should listen to every stupid, pointless thing that comes out of your yaps. That we should all stop and bow down to you just because you're on the rag once a month. We should respect you because you can get knocked up and squirt out some kids. I'm not impressed. I fucking hate kids. I hate the fact that women talk a bunch of shit about wanting to be treated equally, turn around and fuck somebody so they can cut in line, and then try to tell you they're not whores, that it's nobody's business but theirs what they do and who they do it with. Why should tits and ass count for more than brains?"

"That's not a woman's fault," I said. "It's men who made it that way."

"I know," he said. "I hate them too. But they're not as much fun to kill as a chick, and I sure don't want to fuck one."

And then we were quiet, listening to the wind shake the tree tops beyond the end of the parking lot. I was wildly uncomfortable, trying to think of some way, any way to get out of the car. I did not want to be in there with Dave anymore. Not after that.

"I won't hurt you, you know," Dave said. He lit another cigarette and kept staring out the window, into the darkness of the empty bean field behind the hotel. "You've got diplomatic immunity."

"How'd I get so lucky?" I asked.

Dave shrugged. "Lucas seems to like you okay. He hasn't killed you yet, at least."

"What if he wanted to?" I said. "Just hypothetically. What if he was going to kill me? Would you stop him?"

He looked at me, and the old grin was back. "Fuck no."

I laughed so hard I thought I'd pee my pants. Everything was okay again and I was calm. Pregnancy mood swings are a bitch. "You're an asshole," I said.

"Yeah right, blame it on me. It's *Lucas*. What the hell am I supposed to do, jump on his back and ride him until he gets tired? Give me a break."

"You could try to talk him out of it," I said, and we both laughed at that.

The parking lot was quiet. There were a few cars under the pools of light and most of them had PRESS tags hanging from the rearviews. Even under normal circumstances not many people need a motel room in Friedman, Illinois, on a weeknight in October. The weather was good, like a horror movie, a breeze with a touch of chill in it, dead leaves rolling across the parking lot to wherever it is that dead leaves go, some good creepy noises coming from the trees they'd lived on. There weren't any stars and the air smelled like rain.

Dave leaned forward and looked at me. "So what you're really trying to say is that you find me irresistible, that in fact you do want to have wild, passionate sex with me, but the feeling is so overpowering that your inferior intellect won't allow you to express your true feelings in an undiluted form."

Where these things come from, I never have figured out. "I'm saying you're a fucking idiot," I told him.

"We're not talking about me, we're talking about you. These little word games you're playing aren't helping me help you, and that's really what we got into this conversation to do, isn't it?"

I stared at him. "I don't know why we got into this conversation," I said, and I meant it. I wasn't too sure *how* we got into it, either.

He reached a hand between the front seats and put it on top of one of mine, mock-sympathetic, which scared me so bad I almost wet my pants. Lucas is a ninja of sorts, but Dave is no slouch either. I hadn't seen it coming at all. Part of it was the fact that it was dark inside the car, but the rest of it was skill. And those new, bad feelings I'd been having about being trapped alone in the car with Dave came back with a howling vengeance.

"Come on," he said, "don't push me away. This isn't going to get any better if you don't let it out. Share with me. I'm your friend. Your buddy. Your confidant."

I had no idea what he was talking about. All I could think of was him touching me, talking to me in that low, creepy voice, and how small and cramped it was in the backseat of the Lucas' Camaro. How if I screamed, for any reason, nobody would be able to hear me over the rush of the wind. His hand was cool and dry and laying on top of mine, heavy, almost as though it belonged to a dead person.

"You're a pain in my ass," I told him. My bladder felt like it was reaching critical mass and I was afraid to move. I didn't know when being pregnant started messing with your control over your bodily functions, but the passenger seat of Lucas' Camaro was definitely not the place to risk it. If I peed in his car, he probably *would* kill me.

"I think what you're really talking about is the pain you're feeling inside, if only you'd knock down these horrible barriers within yourself and express it."

"Do you want me to punch you?" I said. My voice was

girly and uneven.

"Is it cramps?" Dave smiled. "Is tomorrow's morning sickness starting early? Maybe you have gas."

He was fucking with me, the prick. "I *am* gonna punch you," I told him.

"I see what you're saying," he grinned. "You're in love with me. Don't be afraid. I already know about the baby, and I don't hold it against you. We can get a nanny for Dave Jr., someone who can give him the kind of love and affection he needs until you're able to work these things out and get yourself back on track. But it all begins with that first step, and you're putting that off. Don't do that. Just move that proverbial foot forward and go, sweetheart. It doesn't even have to be your best foot. The club foot with the corns will do for now."

All of that, in that smug Geraldo Rivera-voice of his. It was enough to make you want to tear his throat out. "You're driving me crazy," I said, and jerked my hand out from under his. "You know that, don't you?"

"It's just passion. Don't worry about it. You're shallow. As soon as I have something hanging out of my nose it will pass, and you'll find some other hunk to obsess over."

"That's it," I told him. I clenched my fist in the darkness of my lap, where he couldn't see it. I could be sneaky and fast too, if I wanted to be. At least I hoped so. "You're dead. I'm gonna--"

And then Lucas rapped on the roof with his knuckles and we almost had twin heart attacks. Dave even let out a little strangled yelp, which I made a mental note of so I could be sure to mock him for it later.

"Oh my God!" I said. "What's wrong with you? Do you want to give me a--"

"Room 204," he said through the window.

Dave leaned over the center console to get a better look at him. "Whoa! How'd you find that out?"

"I watch *Scooby-Doo*," Lucas said, his eyes scanning the parking lot in even, sweeping motions.

Dave looked at me and grinned, one of the lot lights glaring across the lenses of his glasses and erasing his eyes. "Who used to be working the desk?" he said.

I noticed for the first time that Lucas was already wearing his black gloves. "L.E.J.A. major," he said. "Let's go."

He headed back toward the hotel as Dave and I crawled out of the car, stretching and groaning with our hair whipping into rat-nest tangles around our ears. We followed him at a distance. "Good thing you didn't go with him," Dave said. "Luke has a thing for L.E.J.A. majors. He likes to cut their dicks off and shove them in their mouths."

That put a falter in my step, for sure. "That's disgusting!" I said.

"Heh," Dave smirked. "You think that's bad, you should see what he does to Business majors."

47

Dave

Sometimes, when I think about heaven and what it will be like when I get there, I get this picture in my head of rows and rows of candy machines, walls of them, everywhere you look. All of them clean and well-lit from the inside, with spotless glass fronts and those big stainless steel corkscrews with the candy bars trapped between the threads, just waiting for you to punch the buttons that will turn the screw and send them dropping to the bottom. The colors of the wrappers will be vibrant, so bright and perfect that you can almost taste them with your eyes. And all the best ones will be there, Snickers and Almond Joys and Mounds and Hershey's with almonds and Nestle's Crunch--the dark, not the white chocolate, which tastes like ass crack--and Whatchamacallits and Kit Kats and Reese's Peanut Butter Cups and NutRageous and all the M&M's. Other kinds too, kinds I've never even heard of, maybe from different planets or universes, or stuff we used to have here on Earth back in the olden days but it got discontinued for some reason.

The stuff wouldn't be free, of course. You'd need quarters to make the machines work, and you'd always have them, because it's Heaven. Part of the fun of a candy machine is sticking your quarters into the slot and listening to them clank down into the machine's guts as a prelude to the soft gear-grinding noise the corkscrews make when they drop your candy with a hollow clanking thud into the bottom of the machine. The creak of the push-panel when you stick your hand through it to grab the stuff. The squeak and clunk of the push-panel coming back home as you remove your hand, the candy in your fist.

Sometimes if I don't have money I like to just stand in front of one of those vending machines and stare into it. It makes me feel good, kind of calm and peaceful. That probably sounds stupid, but if you think about it, how intelligent is it to blank out in front of a TV for hours on end, or drink until you pass out, or take one or more of anything in Lucas' Ziploc bag of magic beans? There's not a lot of good feeling around to be had anymore. You have to take what you can get and make the most of it.

Well, I had money, and on our way through what passed for the hotel lobby en route to Supercunt's room the laundry room door was open and I saw one of those machines inside. It looked nice too, because somebody had turned off all the lights in the room and all you could see was the inside of the machine glowing. It was totally calling my name, and who am I to ignore a little piece of Heaven? So I was trying to decide what to get and wondering why the hell everything had to cost 55¢ now, which is almost as inconvenient as when they raised the price of a pay phone from a quarter so Ma Bell could afford her hysterectomy or whatever the reason was. I'd narrowed it down to a choice between a Snickers and a Mr. Goodbar, which I vaguely remembered liking but hadn't had for a long time, when I heard somebody click-clack into the room behind me on some high heels.

Supercunt.

I know what you're thinking. *Yeah right, asshole. That's a little too convenient, isn't it?*

But it wasn't really all that convenient, because I didn't have my gloves on, or my knife out. And fuck you for calling me an asshole. I watched her reflection in the candy machine's glass front while she tried to smooth out a dollar bill, probably so she could buy a Payday to fuck herself with because she liked the rough feel of salted peanuts scraping her vaginal walls and making them sting. Hey, if that's your thing, whatever. What I can't stand are people who use paper money in vending machines, because that's just ignorant. What jackass thought up that idea, anyway? Obviously somebody who worked for the U.S. Mint, never carried anything but crisp brand-new bills that he kept pressed between the pages of a textbook instead of in his pocket. I'm surprised more murders haven't been committed by God-fearing citizens driven to the brink of insanity by having to wait in line five minutes for some asswipe to smooth out a dollar-bill they've had wadded up in their sweaty crotch since their grandma gave it to them for their last birthday because they suddenly think they need a 3 Musketeers.

I was getting ready to move out of the way and let Supercunt go ahead of me, because I have good candy-machine manners. I was going to butcher her and spread her blood and guts all over a motel room within a half-hour, true, but that's no reason to violate a general principle. With this in mind, I had begun to turn towards her and offer my position in front of the machine when she said, in this total bitch tone of voice:

"Since you obviously don't know what you want, do you mind if I go ahead of you?"

"Yes," I said.

48

Rachel

We were standing in the shadow of an ice machine on the second floor balcony, doing what to me seemed like absolutely nothing. I had begun to wonder if Lucas had somehow figured out how much I hate wait for anything and was making me sit around for long boring periods of time just to drive me insane. And waiting with Lucas is the worst kind of waiting. I couldn't get him to shut up, as usual.

"Where's Dave?" I asked, after a good ten minutes of absolute silence.

He took a drag on his cigarette and nodded toward the stairs near the door to Cindy Dawson's room. "Right there."

She was climbing toward us with Dave right behind her. "Hey!" he said. "What the fuck? You cut in front of me and take the last Snickers and think you're just gonna walk away with it? I was in front of you! Ma'am? Bitch? I'm talking to you. Hey, really. You should give me that."

She was trying to ignore him, but how do you ignore Dave? Once he starts talking it's like having a bad case of mental crabs. "If it's your favorite you should have known what you wanted and gotten out of the way," she said.

"What kind of logic is that?" Dave cried.

She paused and half-turned to him. "If you don't get away from me, I'm calling the police."

"I fucking doubt it," Dave told her.

"I mean it, asshole. I'm calling the police. Do you want to go to jail over a Snickers bar?"

Dave snorted. "Go ahead and call them. I bet they'd be real happy to know how you cut in front of people and steal their candy. I bet they take *you* to jail."

Cindy Dawson pulled her room key out of her pocket and brandished it at him. "I'll use this."

"And do what, unlock me?" Dave said. "That's bad for you, baby. That's like unlocking the cage of a pit bull. I'll try not to hump your leg, but I can't promise I won't poop in front of you."

She unlocked her door and opened it, letting some of the inside light inside spill out. "I mean it! Get away from me!"

"Hey, you're that lady from the TV!" Dave hooted. "Oh wow, I'm really sorry. I was just kidding around."

"Well I don't find it very funny," Cindy Dawson snapped. She turned to go into her room and Lucas moved toward her silently, crushing his cigarette out between his fingers and throwing it over the balcony rail.

"You know what I think is funny?" Dave asked.

She let out a put-upon sigh. "What?"

"When I killed your fucking slut of a sister?" he said. "She pissed all over herself. Now *that's* funny."

I have never seen eyes go that wide, ever. It looked painful. Her mouth dropped open and she sucked for enough air to make her brain function properly, but it was no good. She turned around to run and I was right there, my fist already closing the distance. I broke her nose and dropped her on her Stairmastered ass. There wasn't one of those good wet popping sounds like I've heard when Lucas hits someone in the face, but it still felt good. The ache in my hand made me feel tough as hell.

Lucas grabbed a handful of her styled blonde hair and dragged her into her room, between the foot of the bed and the low dresser-mirror combo that served double-duty as a stand for the TV. *The Addams Family* was playing, I remember that. Lurch destroying a visitor's hat as he announced him.

Dave came in last, closing the door softly behind him, and we stood over her, waiting.

"Oh my God," Cindy Dawson said. Her eyes were watering. *"Oh my God."*

"That's original," Dave snorted. "We've never heard *that* before." He looked at Lucas. "Do you think there's some gene that makes all dumb bitches say the same thing when they're about to be gutted and fucked, or is it just a coincidence?"

"You should know," I said. "You've done enough research."

"Yeah, but I got so turned on reading my notes that all the pages are stuck together," Dave said. "And my tape recorder got blood in it, so that's all fucked up."

"Oh my God," Cindy Dawson moaned. "Don't kill me. I'll give you--"

"Yeah yeah yeah," Dave said. He lit a cigarette. "For someone who takes such pride in being in the public eye, you're not all that bright. I mean, you're faced with your own untimely demise, given a few seconds in which to express what passes for your final thoughts, and this is all you come up with?

"I'm disappointed in you. And that's not a good thing, considering the fact that this can be as quick or as horribly fucking slow and painful as I decide to make it. And? Sounding stupid isn't going to keep me from dating you. It's like a kick in the crotch, you know? It only turns me on more."

"Why?" she cried through her mashed, swollen face. "Why are you doing this?"

"Because we can. And garbage like you should be exterminated before it has a chance to breed."

"She already has two kids," I said.

Lucas was staring at her. "She'll never have a third."

I wish I knew how to describe Lucas in a way that would make you understand. That voice. His eyes when he went into what Dave and I had named the Cobra-Mode. And for all the trash she talked on TV, in the newspapers, and probably even in her sleep about how we couldn't be allowed to go on removing the MTV-brainwashed pillars of the future, once Lucas had locked on her and was in his Cobra-Mode, she was hypnotized. We might as well have darkened the whole room except for a bar of light across his eyes, like Bela Lugosi in *Dracula*, I shit you not.

She started scooting backwards on her unnaturally narrow ass, but there wasn't much exertion in it. It was like she'd taken a bunch of downers and they were just starting to kick in. Sweat and tears had taken a perfectly good makeup job and turned it into some bizarre Halloween costume hybrid of Alice Cooper and a crack whore. She opened her mouth and sucked in breath, preparing to scream.

"Don't." Lucas told her.

"What do I have to *lose?*" she said, with one of those annoying high-pitched whining sounds leaking through at the end. "You're going to kill me anyway!"

"Yeah," Dave said, "but if he crushes your throat and you can't make a sound, he's got the time to work you over all night if he feels like it."

"And he does," I said.

"So shut the fuck up," Dave told her.

She looked back and forth between us, boo-hooing it up, snot running down her upper lip, the whole bit. *"You're all going to burn in hell!"* she screamed.

"Yeah, but at least we'll look good doing it," Dave smirked, and Lucas went for her throat with one of those big vise-grip hands of his.

From the look on her face, that last half-scream must have hurt like a son-of-a-bitch.

"Man," Dave laughed around a fresh cigarette as Lucas switched his knife from his left hand to his right and tested it by slicing the tip of Cindy Dawson's broken-but-still-living nose off. "This is better than the time they stole the other team's goat on *The Brady Bunch.*"

49

<u>Rachel</u>

I woke up in the late afternoon with the whole world on top of me and couldn't shake it off. There was a stale strawberry-and-jasmine incense smell in my apartment that did absolutely nothing for my sinuses and stomach, and it was too quiet there without somebody else's television on. Outside it was gray and damp and chilly and I opened the window a few inches to let it in, wrapping myself from head to toe in every blanket and pillow I had, hoping I would pass out again in my cocoon and sleep dreamlessly for another week, at which point the sun would be shining through my window and I could break out of the cocoon as something else. Something beautiful.

I had missed my Psychology test and maybe another one. Psychology I'd missed for sure, though. I had complete confidence in that particular fact. I tried to remember what the test was on and couldn't; then I tried to recall when I had last been to class, any class, and came up pathetically short. Dave and Lucas are bad influences, and I hadn't exactly been fighting them off.

There are two parts to life. One part is your sense of responsibility, the thing that makes you buckle down and study and plan for your future of a family and kids and a house you can't really afford and a 4-door car that's always at least two years old. It's leaden and dense and dark, like a cannonball, and the weight of it is tricky. At first you pick it up and hold it in your palm and you think that you will be able to keep that hand at waist-height for as long as it takes. Forever, if that's what you have to do.

In the other hand you hold something else entirely. For lack of a more appropriate term, we'll call it the Fuck-All. I'm not exactly sure what *Fuck-All* means, but I've heard

Lucas say it on more than one occasion, and it sounds good when it rolls out of his mouth. The Fuck-All weighs almost nothing, and you don't have to hold it still. The cannonball has to stay at waist-level, but the Fuck-All *needs* to be moving, all the time. It's bright and shiny and full of colors, and it writhes in your fist.

The cannonball makes your arm hurt. It's boring, and when you get bored and sore you get angry at yourself for holding the stupid thing, because you can't remember what the point of your picking it up was in the first place. You look around you and think about all the people you know who picked up the cannonball and devoted themselves to holding it at waist-level. None of them are happy. Their shoulders are rounded, their backs are bent, they are sour and given to complaining for their own entertainment. They believe that life has passed them by. The truth is that at some point in their youth they dropped the Fuck-All and traded it for both hands on the cannonball, the guarantee of a semi-comfortable existence, a spot in the rank-and-file.

Everybody loves the Fuck-All. Without it, there would be no movies, no rock n' roll, no nightly news. Billions of cannonball holders live vicariously through a severe minority, daydreaming about their exploits, trying on different sayings and body languages and mindsets in an attempt to emulate their heroes in some small way. But it doesn't hold up. It *can't* hold up. Because at some point, everything comes down to the choice. The cannonball or the Fuck-All. And once you choose, it's so very difficult to go back. Ask a mobster in the Witness Relocation Program.

Ask a junkie. Ask a rock star who had nothing but cocaine on his glass coffeetable and sluts at his feet for years and now can't get a record deal.

Lying there in my cocoon, I realized that I wasn't making the choice. I was letting the choice make me, which is the worst thing you can do. The direction of your life should not be determined by your own apathy, like a bottle some kid threw into the ocean with a note inside begging whoever finds it to write back and tell him where it ended up. You have to choose. You *have* to. It may turn out good, it may turn out bad, but if you don't choose, the whole thing is worthless.

Like Emilio Zapata said, "It's better to die on your feet than to live on your knees."

And sometimes it's better to lay around in your little cocoon and feel sorry for your pregnant self than to get up and do something. At least it seems that way at the time. I rolled over, buried my face in the pillow, and tried to sleep, but I was done. I got up with the blankets still wrapped around me and set up fort on the couch in front of the TV.

I don't know why I did it. Maybe because there was nothing on but talk shows with teenage girls taking their eighth paternity test and people cheating on each other and horribly deformed children. Maybe because I needed a change of scenery. Maybe I just needed to get laid. But I got up, dropped the blankets, and started taking down the clippings I'd tacked to the wall behind the television set. I stacked them all in a neat pile on top of the VCR until the wall was a blank piece of paper, covered with invisible sentences and punctuated with tack-holes. The story of my life.

Who am I kidding?

That's the story of everyone's life.

50

<u>Rachel</u>

I went over to the house around 4:30. As soon as I opened the back door something felt wrong; when I got to the living room I realized the television was off. That was a new one. Even when those idiots went to bed they left the stupid thing on, for some reason. They were sitting in the living room, smoking, staring off into space. It didn't even look like they knew the other one was in the room.

"What's up?" I said.

Dave looked at me and flipped the envelope in his hand across the room like a Frisbee. It landed on a pile of other junk mail, magazines and homework assignments, and as soon as I blinked I couldn't tell which one it had been.

"The school sent me a letter," Dave said. "Fuck. If I don't get my grades up by the end of the semester, I'm out."

"That's not going to happen, is it?" I said.

"No."

I kicked the toe of Lucas' boot. "I'm guessing your grades aren't any better," I said.

"Fuck grades," he yawned, and picked up the thick biography of Heinrich Himmler that was already open on his lap.

"At least in prison I can't skip class," Dave said, and guzzled beer.

"And they'll make you shower once a week," I smiled.

He didn't smile back.

"You know what you guys need?" I said.

Dave looked at me. "Sex?"

"Uh, no," I said. "Well, maybe. You guys need to go out and act like normal people. Hang out with someone besides each other."

"I think the sex idea is better."

"I'm serious. Don't you guys ever go out drinking or something?"

Dave made a face. "I don't think that's such a good idea."

"Why not?" I said. "It'll do you good."

"It sounds good in theory--" Dave began.

"To her maybe," Lucas said.

"Think of all the worthless people you can find," I told them. "It'll be like going to the toy store when you're a kid."

Lucas looked at me with no expression at all.

"I think you're barking up the wrong tree," Dave smirked.

"He never went to the toy store when he was a kid?"

"No." Lucas said.

"Jesus, what kind of fucked up childhood did you have?" I asked.

Dave snorted. "Considering the end result you see before you, I'm not sure that question dignifies a reply."

He had a point.

"Let's just go," I said. "You guys will have a good time, I swear."

"Bet your life on it?" Dave grinned.

"No way."

"Why not?"

"Because you assholes would collect," I said.

No one disagreed with me.

51

<u>Dave</u>

Pete and I always liked going to the bar--it was Lucas who hated it. If the planets were lined up perfectly, in that special formation that looks like they're giving God the finger, we could get him to go, but he never liked it. Actually, it was always more fun when Lucas went, because then we could count how many people turned around and looked at him and dropped their drinks, which always amused us to no end, because we're assholes.

Going to the bar is what I like to refer to as dyslexic fun. Most people go to the bar to socialize and pick up the chicks and try to get laid and dance and all that crap. I, on the other hand, go there and pretend I like to do these things. The fun part comes when, after you've insinuated yourself into the crowd, and you've met someone new who thinks you're fun to hang out with, you start doing something fucked up and make them mad or freak them out or whatever. So it's like, you're there to have fun, but your fun is the reverse of everyone else's fun. *Dyslexic* fun. Get it?

I don't know how she talked Lucas into going with, but she did. Feminine charms or a blowjob, I guess, which are basically the same thing. He looked as happy to be there as he looks to be anywhere else, which is not that happy. We had to stand in line outside before we could get in, and pay a $5 cover because there was a shitty industrial band playing. We could hear their stench all the way out on the sidewalk, which I thought made it a good opportunity to warm-up a little bit and give my dance moves one last run-through before I got in there with the ladies. I tried to get a mosh pit going right there on the sidewalk, but nobody else was into it, and they got really pissed off when I kept slamming into them and screaming *"Satan loves you, dude!"* Finally I had to go stand beside Lucas and bum a cigarette off him so all those frat rats could see that kicking my ass was probably not the best way to start off the evening.

When we got up to the door, some fat kid with a mustache and his gut sucked in was taking the cover and stamping hands. "I saw you back there," he said. He actually had braces, with some weird aqua-colored plastic in them, and he was like 23. Jesus Christ. "You better not start any trouble inside, or we'll put your head through the wall."

"Like a glory hole?" I said. "You'll put my head through the wall and then suck it, so you don't have to face the shame of avoiding my eyes when you see me later with your heterosexual friends around?"

Bouncer Boy opened his mouth to say something stupid back, I'm sure, but Lucas pinched me on the ass so hard that I jumped through the door and yelled, and the whole thing was over. Lucas paid the cover for all of us, probably because he was the only one who had any money.

The place was packed in asshole-to-elbow, as I've heard Lucas say. He does not like crowded places. He does not like people touching him, deliberately or otherwise. Fortunately for Lucas, he puts off such a general bad vibe that anybody who isn't completely wasted out of their head picks up on it and backs off to give him space, even when it means crushing awkwardly against someone else. This is why you always let him go first. He can cut through a crowd in two seconds flat.

I'd been in that particular shithole a few times, because they had 75¢ drafts on Tuesday nights and the chicks who went there were usually really slutty looking. You walked straight in to the bar, which was up against a wall with no stools and some shaky, leaning tables and chairs scattered around it. If you turned left you went into the back where the pool tables and dart boards were, which was where the jocks, frat rats, and redneck townies trying to pick up some college snatch hung out. There was a door back there that led out to the fenced-in beer garden, but it was only open in the early fall and late spring. If you turned right and walked through a totally useless wall that was about four feet high and took three steps down--always a bright architectural idea to have steps in any building where you plan to serve disgusting amounts of alcohol to binge drinkers--there was a dance floor with a DJ booth on one end and a stage on the other. It was the only bar in town that ever had industrial music, so there were always a bunch of wannabe vampire kids running around with a bunch of metal shit in their faces smelling like strawberry incense and clove cigarettes.

All those kids were on the dance floor thrashing around and sweating all over each other because this totally shitty Marilyn Manson rip-off band was onstage defiling the history of music. They had this big white bloody-looking sheet hung up behind them with the word **SLUTCUTTER** spray painted on it, and under that *67 and counting...*

Lucas had gone to get drinks, but Rachel was standing next to me. "I don't get it," I yelled in her ear. "Sixty-seven what? Girls that have refused to sleep with them? Record labels that laughed in their faces? How many times they've pierced their genitalia?"

She looked at me like the idiot I probably am. "It's the body count," she yelled back.

I thought about that. Nothing came to mind. I shrugged.

Her eyes darted around to see if anybody might be listening, as if you could hear anything over the crap coming through the PA. "That serial killer?" she said, giving me quit-being-stupid eyebrows. "I think that's the body count."

This was confusing to me, to say the least. I personally had never kept track of things like that, because seriously, who gives a rat's ass? Once we killed them they were nothing more than maximum-Catholic-guilt masturbation fantasies, for me anyway. Now, on an entirely different and more disturbing level, although with obvious parallels, a quintet of jerk-offs had co-opted our hard earned reputation for madness, mayhem, and all manners of depravity and were trying to make a buck off of it. Talk about your disgusting concepts.

The band ended one song and started another. At least I think they did. They were so awful that it was hard to be certain. Lucas came back with the drinks--Long Island Iced Tea for himself, Coke for Rachel because she was preggers, and an Amaretto Stone Sour for me, because it amuses me to drink like a soratory chick until I get impatient with the joke and start doing shots and chugging Natty Lights.   Lucas, of course, knew exactly what **67 and counting...** meant, because as we all know at this point, he is truly the bastard son of Satan, and doesn't miss a trick. This is both good and bad when you take into account the fact that he absolutely despises tricks.

Some dorky looking Math major-type kid with black clothes and corn starch all over his face managed to get the attention of the singer, who you could tell was totally into Green Day and the Offspring in junior high and probably spent a lot of homo-erotic bonding time with his "buds," fucking up skateboard tricks in suburban public places and talking like he'd been born and raised in the inner city. They had a little Trent Reznor fan club meeting and the singer stopped the band, jumping up and down he was so excited.

"Hey, shut the fuck up!" he screamed into the microphone, an old trick he'd picked up from watching tapes of Frank Sinatra, no doubt. "They just said on the news that the cunt they found in that hotel room was Cindy

Dawson! They fucking slaughtered her and some other guy! It's number 69! *Number 69!"*

And then it seemed like the whole place was screaming its lungs out. Cheering. For us. And it didn't stop. No exaggeration, it must have gone on for a good three or four minutes. My ears hurt, my whole head throbbed.

"Hell yeah," the singer said. "In honor of another victory for the good guys--"

More cheering. More back slapping. More wild, drunken adrenaline. Somebody got a can of spray paint and began changing *67* to *69* on the sheet behind the band.

We left.

Lucas stopped at the liquor store and got us each a bottle of Aristocrat vodka after we dropped Rachel off at her apartment. She didn't even say anything, just got out of the car, looked back at us once, and went inside. As soon as her door was closed and her light went on, we opened our bottles and chugged. For the first time I was so angry that I felt dangerous to myself, and that feeling made me horrified, from the roots of my hair to the tips of my toes and back again.

52

Rachel

"They were cheering," I said. We were sitting in one of Lucas' out-of-the-way, hole-in-the-wall diner-type restaurants.

No one said anything. I ripped open three packets of

Equal and dumped them out on the formica table top, swirling designs in the mess with the tip of my pinky. "They were *cheering*," I said again.

Dave was slouched in his section of the horseshoe booth, slightly hungover, hands tucked flat under his arms, eyebrows locked in a contemplative V over the bridge of his nose. He was smiling, but not happily. Dave has a smile for almost every occasion, not unlike the Joker on the old *Batman* TV show. "There's something really wrong with that, but I can't quite put my finger on it."

"Maybe that we've become our own little Hicksville pop culture phenomena?" I said. I made a smiley face in the sweetener and cut slashes into it with my thumbnail. "It's a good thing we didn't have any kind of message we were trying to put across. We would have screwed that up royally."

Dave was rocking slightly from the waist, like a homeless person on a park bench. "I think you screwed up royally as soon as you took us to a bar full of frat rats and Marilyn Manson fans. We might have to duct tape you to a chair and get some religious guy to yell at you for six or seven hours like they do those teenage Satan worshipping kids who take shop class."

"Deprogramming?" I offered.

"It's got nothing to do with TV," he said. I couldn't tell if he was kidding or not. "Would you try to stay on the subject here?"

"The subject being teenage devil worshippers who take shop class?" I asked.

"Or the fact that I just ordered two hamburgers and don't have any money," he said. "Whose turn is it to pay for me?"

Both of us turned to Lucas. "Don't look at me," he said. "I paid the last 98 times."

Dave punched me in the shoulder. Not hard enough to hurt, really, but harder than is commonly acceptable to hit the shoulder of a pregnant girl. "I guess that leaves you, baby," he said. "Hope you brought your credit card, because I'm thinking about dessert."

"I'm thinking more along the lines of you getting a job so you can pay for your own fucking hamburgers," I said.

"Would you hire me?"

"Hell no."

"Then shut up and pay for my goddamn hamburgers," he said. "If you're gonna be part of the problem, you'd better be prepared to be part of the solution." He looked at Lucas. "So what do we do about this?"

"How come you never ask me for any ideas?" I said. I'd jammed my hand into my pants pocket to see how much money I had and it was sort of stuck there. I'd been putting off buying bigger pants because I was still in denial about the whole you're-pregnant-and-your-ass-is-getting-fatter thing.

Dave gave me one of those *yeah, right* looks and opened his mouth to say something else.

"What?" I said, cutting him off. "I'm not smart enough to be in your cool little inner circle?"

"How can it be a circle if there's only two of us?"

"You know what I mean," I said, and managed to yank my hand out of my pants before my circulatory system was permanently damaged.

"I know you need to work on your geometry," Dave said.

"I'm serious. You guys never ask me for ideas."

They stared at me.

"What?" I said.

"What's your idea?" Lucas said.

"I'm not saying I have one right this second--"

Dave snorted. "Well thank God you interrupted the flow of things so we could listen to you rant about feeling unloved. I'd hate to think I might have lived the rest of my life without ever knowing that."

"You are such an *asshole*," I hissed at him.

"That wraps up the minutes of the last meeting, now on to new business. Luke, any thoughts?"

Lucas was staring out the window, looking at whatever it is someone like him finds interesting. "None that don't involve a machine gun and a lot of ammo," he said. His eyes never left the window.

"See?" I said. "He doesn't have any great ideas either."

"Are you still here?" Dave said. "Shouldn't you be listening to Tori Amos in a room full of lit candles and writing really bad poetry you'd just *die* if anyone saw?"

"Shouldn't you be taking the third shower of your life?" I said.

"Oooh," he grinned. A real one. "This is getting interesting. Shouldn't you be--"

"Could we do this later?" Lucas said, his eyes still out the window. "I'm kind of trying to think here."

Dave poked me in the ribs. "You're fucking lucky, baby," he said. "He pulled your fat out of the fire. *This time.*"

I poked him back and smiled. "Asshole."

53

<u>Dave</u>

Lucas had taken over Pete's room, but he hadn't really done much with the place. Of course, his interior decorating skills involve taking someone's interior and decorating the walls with it--which is nice to do in somebody else's place, but, according to Lucas, too smelly and drab to do at home. The huge plant pots were still there and full of dirt, but Pete's plants were all dead, and the room still smelled like vanilla candles, but the scent was fading, and mostly just smelled like old wax. Even that seemed to be dying off, because Lucas has this thing about keeping a window open, even if only a crack, unless it's below zero or rain is blowing in. He does it in his car too, which is always nice for the sucker riding in the back seat in winter.

It's hard to say just how much stuff Lucas does or doesn't have, because his possessions seem to be in a constant migratory pattern. He has things and then he doesn't have them, and when you ask what happened to them, he's always vague about it. The concept of Lucas being vague on any subject is a real mind-bender, I know, but try to wrap your brain around it. Books and CDs are basically all he ever keeps around, a few clothes and a typewriter. He sleeps with one blanket and makes his bed by rolling it up commando-style and laying it at the head of the bed next to his pillows.

One good thing about Lucas is that you can basically do whatever you want in his room, and he doesn't care. Pete, on the other hand, was a total cunt about it. He had all these bullshit rules--don't leave anything of yours in his room when you leave, don't put your feet on the bed with your shoes on, don't smoke on the bed, don't tap your ashes in a half-full Mountain Dew can on the floor and then accidentally kick it over so the syrupy-black sludge stains the lime green carpet, don't pour beer in the plants--on and on and on.

Since Rachel had dragged us to the bar Lucas had been even more quiet than usual, which is hard to explain, since he basically never says shit anyway. You could sense it in the air, this feeling that all the stuff inside him that constantly analyzes and dissects the outside world had taken a 180° turn and was all focused inside while he thought over what, if anything, we should do next.

Personally, I was excited. Partly because we hadn't gone trick-or-treating in a while and I was starting to get bored with plain old jerking off again, and partly because I knew that Lucas was absolutely *pissed off*. We were being exploited. Bloodthirsty sociopath though he may be, Lucas can't stand exploitation of any sort, unless it's one of those shitty drive-in movies he's always watching.

So I was sitting on the bed, putting gray shoeprints on Lucas' black sheet, leaning on his rolled-up blanket and pillows, smoking one of his cigarettes, tapping the ashes in a third-full Mountain Dew can that was teetering on the mattress beside me, and drinking a bottle of his Corona that I would occasionally spit a mouthful of into the massive pot full of dirt beside the bed.

Take that Pete, you dead fuck.

Lucas had the closet door open and was looking at the spines of a row of paperbacks about mass murderers and serial killers, of which he has several at any given time. Some of them are good enough to keep, but most of those kinds of books are horrifically lacking in anything that even vaguely resembles literary nutrition, so there's a pretty high turnover rate in that section of his library. It doesn't matter much. He remembers at least 80% of everything he reads once anyway. I think he just keeps them for the pictures.

"What are you doing?" I asked. I knew what he was doing; I was just looking for an excuse to say something that I would find amusing while reminiscing about the situation an hour later, as I am prone to do.

"Thinking."

"Still? Jesus. I never did anything for that long, except masturbate. For some reason I had this weird fantasy where I was in the ice cream truck from the Smashing Pumpkins' video with Winnie Cooper and Sabrina the Teenage Witch, and I'd be, you know, thinking about them, but then every time I'd get ready to, *you know,* I'd start wondering if there was some new kind of ice cream bar in the truck I hadn't tasted and then I'd lose my place and have to start all over again."

I couldn't see Lucas' face, but under that heavy-metal-biker mane of his, I could tell the back of his skull was giving me its rapt attention. "Did you actually read all those books?" I asked him, even though I knew fucking good and well that he had. For Lucas, an unread book lying around is like getting out of your car in the Wal-Mart parking lot and leaving the door open.

"Yeah."

"More than once?"

"Yeah," he said.

At least that was marginally interesting. I mean, who would re-read serial killer books? That takes a very distinct personality type. I'm sure even a closed-minded boob like you wouldn't argue with that.

"Awesome," I said. "Give you any good ideas?"

"Nothing original."

I finished my beer and whipped the bottle out into the other part of the basement, where it shattered off the corner of the dryer with a really cool sound. Lucas looked at me and nodded, impressed. "Speaking of unoriginal," I told him, "they had that singer stroke on TV today."

He turned to me, hands clasped behind his back. A position not unlike something you could imagine an Abraham Lincoln or a Thomas Jefferson standing in. "Why?"

"I guess they're getting hard up for new stories. Apparently a bunch of labels are talking about signing them."

"Really," he said. Almost like he was talking to himself.

"Yeah. Some former county fair queen was asking him if he didn't feel bad about trying to make a career out of glorifying something as fucked-up as us."

"As opposed to what she and every other jerk-off with a suit and a microphone are trying to do," he said, which was a point I hadn't considered. "What'd he say?"

"*Dude,*" I mocked. "Serial killers are *awesome.*"

That one-sided smirk I hadn't seen for way too long slid onto Lucas' face, and I felt good. Really good. Like you're 13 years old and Santa brings you a 12 year-old chick with huge tits who thinks you're the hottest thing that ever walked the earth, is a nymphomaniac, doesn't begin to understand the concept of the word "no," and tells you that your parents are dead, they were secretly millionaires, and they've left you everything. That kind of good.

"And where does this Gen-X John Lennon live?" Lucas asked.

"I don't know," I said, grinning so hard my face hurt. "But I bet we can find out."

54

Rachel

It was one of those really great days, weather-wise, the kind you know you'll keep in the back of your head like a photograph so you can bring it out and look at it in your old age, when your own eyes aren't so good. The sky was brilliant blue, full of puffy white clouds with the perfect amounts of silver-gray in them; the leaves on the trees were as colorful as they would ever be and gently falling in the breeze; the sun was on its afternoon downhill slide, not so bright you couldn't give it a brief look if you wanted to, and throwing a perfect golden light on any surface that would accept it. The weather affects me, whatever it may be. There is no reason for it that I know, and no way I can stop it. And yeah I had problems and yeah a lot of things at that moment seemed to have purchased a one-way ticket to Shitsville and yeah I was a vile, murdering cunt, but I felt *good*.

I was always asking Lucas for rides by that point, to doctor's appointments and to the grocery store and pretty much everywhere I needed to go, except for classes. He never complained about it. I'd call the house and leave a message on the machine--they never answered the phone, as far as I knew--that I had an appointment at such-and-such time, and a half hour before I needed to be there I'd hear three sharp raps on the door, and there would be Lucas. Winston Light hanging from the corner of his mouth, his hair sometimes still damp from the shower and the razor-cuts on his jaw line sometimes still clotting, but he'd be there.

We were sitting on a stone bench outside the county hospital, waiting for my appointment, which was scheduled for 2:30 and probably wouldn't start until after 4:00. They were always backed up, and then had the nerve to seem indignant about it, as if any ailment that didn't fit into their regimented 10-minutes-per-patient schedule was a sure sign that the world was full of whiny assholes. They were always making me wait when I went in by myself, which was another reason I liked to have Lucas with me. Nobody wanted him in their waiting room. He made the whole place uncomfortable, which is admirable in and of itself, in my book. Who do you know that can go into a room of sick, hurt, self-absorbed people and with absolutely no effort make them focus on something other than their own problems?

"Almost time to go in," I said. I hated to say anything, because the day was beautiful and I had begun to appreciate that you could sit next to someone and be silent without there being animosity between you.

Lucas sucked in on his cigarette, his lips making a small crackling sound as they disengaged from the filter. "Not me," he said. The smoke that carried the words from his mouth was beautiful.

"Don't feel like playing dad again?" I smiled, but I was disappointed. I really wanted him to be there.

"I don't want to look at that," he said. Maybe even gently.

"Thanks a lot," I told him. "Getting a little squeamish, are we?"

One corner of his mouth went up and his head turned slightly in my direction, his eyes impossible to see behind the sunglasses. "I may be a bloodthirsty animal, but I've got morals."

"You don't mind watching Dave date a dead girl, but

seeing me get a necessary medical exam offends you?" I asked, more than a little offended myself.

"I never said the morals were perfect."

I will never understand male squeamishness when it comes to menstruation and other matters of the female reproductive system. Guys are programmed to want pussy, pussy, pussy, but mention something about having your period, or cramps, or PMS, or God forbid, anything about tampons or maxi-pads, and it's like shoving a crucifix in Dracula's face. It's like having a very special strain of leprosy that only flares up five days a month. The word *gynecologist* alone will make some of them wince in disgust. We live the so-called Information Age, where everything there is to know on the subject is shoved down your throat beginning in fifth grade health class and then continues on in 3 out of 5 television commercial breaks, and the majority of men would still rather be mugged at gunpoint than purchase a box of Tampax at Wal-Mart.

"What's the matter, afraid to see my best side?" I smiled, and forced myself not to drop my eyes. "I'd show you, you know."

"Christ," he muttered.

I scooted over to erase the few inches of distance between us and draped my arm around the back of his neck, nuzzling his ear before softly breathing into it "Come on, you don't have to play hard to get. It's not like I'm gonna get pregnant or anything."

He planted his fingers on the front lip of the stone bench and rose to his feet, the sweet herbal shampoo smell of his hair still in my nose. "I'm outta here," he said, and started off in the direction of the car.

"Wait!" I called after him, trying not to laugh. "Are you coming back to pick me up?"

He didn't look back. "No."

"Liar!" I yelled. It echoed off the hard, chilly surfaces all around the bench, making me jump and giving birth to a shiver in the center of my spine that ran in both directions at once.

55

Rachel

He came back to get me, of course. He even took me to the Dairy Queen and stood in line with me while I got a crunch-cone, which may be the greatest faux-food ever invented in the history of humankind. He bought my cone and a box of Buster Bars for Dave, and we headed back to the house. I kept pretending to be interested in the plethora of colorful pamphlets bestowed upon me by the highly competent staff at the hospital in the hopes that he would ask me something, anything about my condition.

He didn't, of course.

Dave was rummaging through the odds and ends of the fridge when we came through the back door. Lucas held up the box of Buster Bars to get his attention and then flipped it at him like a Frisbee. It bounced off Dave's chest and he made a lucky grab that kept it off the floor.

"Fantastic," he said. "These are the ones with the fudge

and peanuts in them, correct?"

Lucas guided him away from the fridge with one hand and took out a bottle of beer.

"So what's the word?" Dave asked, already tearing into the plain brown box. "Is it gonna be a dog or a goat?"

"Dave," I said. "So nice to see you. Eating again?"

He ripped the white paper wrapping off the first Buster bar with his teeth and spat it in the general direction of the trashcan, which was empty only because I'd changed the bag in it the day before. "I'm a growing boy," he said.

"You act like a 12 year-old," I told him.

"You've got tits like a 12 year-old," he grinned. "Maybe we can do our homework together."

"I do not have tits like a 12 year-old!" I said.

"Does that mean you're not gonna do my homework?" he frowned.

Lucas held the bottle cap between his thumb and middle finger and snapped, sending it into the trashcan like a bullet. He took three massive swallows that removed half of the beer from the bottle and belched silently. "Did you find out where that kid lives?"

"What kid?" I asked.

"The one from the club who was cheering for us," Dave said. "Marilyn Hanson."

"Why are you trying to find him?"

Dave smirked. "I think Luke wants to pose him for some publicity photos."

"I take it he won't have to worry about being blinded by flashbulbs," I said.

"Or by a big white light, considering the fact that he's an industrial kid and therefore going straight to hell," Dave said. He gnawed into the Buster Bar and winced at the cold on his teeth.

I glanced at Lucas. "Should I ask?"

"Probably not."

"I didn't know where to look for him," Dave shrugged.

Lucas took another swallow and lit a cigarette, one corner of his mouth moving, or maybe not. "Why didn't you just look in the phone book?"

Dave took another bite, this time getting cold fudge around the corners of his mouth. He crunched peanuts and looked at us. "Jesus I'm a fucking idiot."

56

Rachel

Dave wanted to go to the party. Dave practically *begged* to go to the goddamn party. But Lucas said it had to be me, that I was the one who could blend in and do what needed to be done, if anything. Personally, I think he was just throwing down payback for me wanting to go to the bar in the first place, but I couldn't prove it.

It turned out that Slutcutter, the crappy industrial nü-metal band from the bar, had actually managed to sign a record deal. There's nothing more comforting than realizing that a third party with no original thoughts or talent can still somehow exploit both the hard work and misery of others for their own personal gain, all without getting their hands dirty. And before you go accrediting that particular thought to me and start expecting things like that to fly out of my brain all the time, let me admit that it's more or less a direct quote from Lucas, who accepted my appreciation of it with a nod and then told me to go read *The Fountainhead*.

Lucas was not pleased about this sudden turn of events. At all. I don't know how you would label it--angry, irritated, upset, annoyed, irked--none of those words seems to do the trick the way it should. And if Dave hadn't mentioned it I probably wouldn't have known, because apparently, when Lucas gets pissed off, all he does is smile a lot. Very strange. When I asked Dave why this was, he said, "I have no idea. I've always assumed it's because he's imagining what he's going to do about it, and he finds killing and destroying things to be highly amusing."

So anyway, Slutcutter was all set to be the Next-Big-Shitty-Mass-Marketed-Thing, and they were having a house party to celebrate it. Lucas had scouted the house out and knew everything about it but how much they were paying for electricity. I got into the party with no trouble, mingled with a bunch of drug-addled losers and sluts with too much mascara, stood in line for the bathroom most of the night, and pretended to drink the same cup of beer. Slutcutter played, way too long and way too loud, with too much anti-witty banter between songs.

They could definitely rock the house. If it was their own house and full of their friends, anyway. It was not a pleasant evening. The outside of my head was constantly being gang-raped by that shitty music and the inside was burning Lucas in effigy for making me go in the first place, which blistered me up nicely and left him untouched. And to be fair to the genius of the situation, he didn't *make* me go. He *told* me to go, yes. If I had refused, he might have blinked at me once before setting me aside like a lawn chair and going on with his mowing.

So I stumbled around the place as best I could, pushing my way from room to room and trying to figure out what it was I was supposed to be doing. "You'll know," he'd said when I asked him.

"What if I don't?" I'd said.

"Then don't do anything," Dave told me. "And for chrissakes, don't go around blowing everybody just because it's a party. If you get those warts around your mouth again, I'm gonna have to call Children and Family Services to take your baby away, as soon as it's born, and you won't even get to hold it."

I'd grabbed a claw-hammer off their tiny kitchen table and tried to cave his skull in with it, but Lucas caught my wrist and twisted it just enough to make me drop the hammer without hurting me. The big sweetie. Considering that he probably could have broken my wrist like a bird's neck without even thinking about it, it was almost enough to make me think he really cared about me. I might have too, if he would have stopped laughing, the asshole.

I used to like parties, I think. Or I liked the *idea* of parties. Actual parties ruin that for me. They're hot, they're stuffy, they're poorly ventilated and full of too many kinds of smoke--tobacco, marijuana, clove, incense, candles. Too much aftershave, hairspray and perfume. Beer sweat and patchouli. The beer is warm, the line for the bathroom is too long, and people only talk to the people they came to the party with. The music is always shitty and somebody always wants to play some jackass drinking game. Some girl is always crying. People say things that aren't funny and expect you to laugh. Guys you don't like who have been watching you from afar get drunk enough to decide to finally go for it and express their undying love for you, in front of others.

I bumped into Fritz, the Biology grad assistant, while I was standing in the endless line for the bathroom. More to the point, he saw me from across the room and wove his way through the crowd after the first band set. He made eye contact and held it for way too long. I looked away; when I looked back he was closer and still staring, and you could tell he'd totally been practicing this James Bond bullshit in the mirror since he was like 14.

"Hi," he said. He leaned in closer than he needed to and I could feel his warm breath tickling my ear. "How are you?"

I nodded at him and let my eyes go a little wide and then normal again.

"You look bored," he said, in my ear again, then leaned back and smiled wryly, like it was a private joke between us.

"I was bored," I told him.

He smiled wider. "And now?"

I smiled back. "Now I'm catatonic."

His smile faltered. "How's the tutoring coming along?"

he said.

It took me a second to figure out what he was talking about--not only had I forgotten about finding a Bio tutor, I'd basically stopped going to class. On the days I did go I found myself daydreaming about motherhood and eviscerating the prof.

"Oh, good," I nodded. "It's going well, thanks."

"Who'd you end up with?" he said, and pressed up against me to let somebody pass, even though they already had more than enough room.

"Is your wife here?" I said, looking over his shoulder.

He grinned. "No, my *fiancé* is running the coffeehouse tonight," he said. "Why? What'd you have in mind?"

"I was hoping to borrow a pad," I told him, and tried to sound solemnly sincere. "I haven't seen any girls I know here, and mine really needs to be changed."

"Oh," he said, already backing away.

"That doesn't make you uncomfortable, does it?" I asked. "I mean, usually I wouldn't, you know, but with you in Bio and all--"

"No, it's cool," he nodded, still backing away. "I saw some girls from the coffeehouse in the living room, I'll go ask around and get back to you if I find anything, okay?"

I didn't see him again all night.

57

Dave

Marilyn Hanson was probably my least favorite. It was

kind of like we *had* to do it, and there was more or less an organized plan of sorts, so it was basically like a job. I do not understand, accept, or approve of chores, jobs, or work in any way, shape, or form. Some would say that makes me a lazy person. And to these judgmental pricks I would say that if these are the kind of pointless, negative thoughts you're going to come up with in your free time, it's probably a good thing that you don't have much of said free time. Keep taking it up the ass, doing a bunch of stupid crap you don't give a flying fuck about for some idiot you daydream about killing so that you can earn money to buy things you don't really need to impress people you don't like and bribe the people you secretly blame for holding you down into pretending they love and respect you. You're an empty, gutless shell of a human being who will die wretched and unsatisfied just like me. The only difference is that I understand this and don't particularly care. And if I wanted to kill my boss, I'd probably just do it and get it over with, because seriously, what the fuck do I care about him living? It's not like he (or she) would be making the quality of my life any better.

We ended up in the kitchen drinking Marilyn Hanson's Coronas, which I found hidden in the fridge behind a Tupperware bowl of this really good pasta salad with black olives and ranch dressing of some kind in it. I hopped up on the counter to eat some of it and landed in a puddle of spilled keg beer, which soaked right into the ass of my khakis and did nothing to improve my disposition. The kitchen had one of those swinging doors, and since I was closest to it, I could hear the host herding the last of his guests out the door.

"If you get a chance you should try to find out how he makes this salad," I said. "This is probably one of the five best pasta salads I've ever eaten."

Lucas' head cocked slightly to the side. "What's in it?"

I poked around in the bowl with a fork I'd found in one of the drawers. "Black olives, maybe some pimentos. It's got ranch flavor, but not like a dressing or something. Probably a mix." I hooked a green grape with the tines of the fork and flicked it out onto the floor. "And grapes, but what moron puts grapes in a pasta salad?"

Lucas blinked a couple of times, like he was rolling that over in his mind. But probably not. "Take the fork with you," he said, and I could tell by the look in his eyes that he wasn't really with me on the whole pasta salad problem anymore.

Somebody turned the stereo off in the living room and I could hear a couple of chicks giggling. It sounded weird in the new silence, but I had to admit that weird slut laughter was an improvement over KORN. I pushed the kitchen door with the toe of my shoe and looked through the crack. "We do a *lot* of stuff together," the first Raging Whore was saying.

I leaned forward to see who she was talking to. Marilyn Hanson, natch. That little douchebag had two chicks in there, just slutting around waiting on him to hump them, can you believe that? I mean, seriously, what the fuck is this world coming to when a scrawny no-talent poser piece of human feces like that gets two chicks and me, his inspiration, gets to sit in a puddle of piss-warm beer eating pasta salad with green grapes in it?

Anyway.

"We do a *lot* of stuff together," the Raging Whore #1 said.

"Anything I'd like to watch?" Marilyn Hanson said, because after all, the guy was suave and debonair.

"Oh *definitely*," Raging Whore #2 giggled.

"And a few things that require audience participation," Raging Whore #1 said.

Goddamn it. I know this story isn't turning out to be easy to follow the way I'm telling it, but everything about it pisses me off, and I'm not one to let things that piss me off just slide by unnoticed when I can sit around and bitch about them.

Who says things like this? Do normal people--the rank and file of the human race, so to speak--actually just let this utter crap fall out of their mouths and think it means anything? Or is it just Americans? Maybe speakers of the English language in general. Because I can imagine it coming out of some equally vapid British kids who listen to too much club music or something, but what about Chinese kids, or West Africans? The fact that clichéd drivel like this passes for human interaction, let alone foreplay, is living proof of what happens when a society makes a habit of catering to the lowest-common-*Girls-Gone-Wild* denominator.

You know what? The hell with this. I'm sick of

thinking about it again already, so let's just hit the highlights, shall we?

Something was said about making sure that nobody had drowned in the toilet and Marilyn Hanson went around the house turning off all the lights. Apparently the romantic mood he was trying to establish was going to benefit greatly if the Raging Whores couldn't see him or the beer-soaked spilled ashtray he lived in.

You have to admit, it couldn't hurt.

He swung the kitchen door open and saw Lucas sitting at the table, drinking the last of the Coronas.

"What's up my man?" he said to Lucas with a forced, hey-I'm-a-cool-guy smile.

Lucas blew smoke. "Not much."

Marilyn Hanson looked at the collection of empty Corona bottles on the table and made a face, but didn't mention them. To paraphrase the answer to an age-old riddle, a 500-lb. gorilla can drink as many of your special beers as he wants. "I don't wanna be a dick or nothing, but the party's over, bro. Everybody split."

Lucas emptied the bottle into his throat and set it down. He was giving Marilyn Hanson the old snake eyes, and I reached for the butcher knife I'd scavenged out of one of the drawers.

"I saw your band the other night," he said. Very polite, conversational.

"Oh yeah?" Marilyn Hanson grinned. "What'd you think?"

"My friend saw you on TV."

I slid down quiet, so my feet were on the floor and my back was still against the counter to use for leverage in case the little douche decided to run for it. The butcher knife had a weird handle and a cheap, shitty blade and it didn't feel right. I was sick of drinking Corona but I still had a bottle in my hand, a backup in case the knife crumpled up on me.

Marilyn Hanson was beginning to get nervous. He let out a fake snorting, surprised kind of laughing bark and pointed at Lucas--a motion I have never really felt compelled to try, even as part of a joke. "We had class together, right?" Marilyn Hanson tittered. "We're you in Stevenson's 20th Century American Lit with me?"

How lame can you get? As if the fact that both of you had to read *My Antonia* and take an essay test over its deep hidden meanings is enough common ground to build anything on.

"We've been seeing you all over the place," Lucas told him, and Marilyn Hanson glanced back at me for the first time. He was scared, but it was nothing spectacular. Even that guy's expressions were fucking unoriginal and boring. "And every time, you're talking about the same fucking thing," Lucas was telling him. "Us."

The two and two got to four, but it took about ten seconds longer than it should have. And then he bolted like a bunny rabbit, through the swinging kitchen door and into the living room. I was closer but Lucas had anticipated it and was already up and moving, across the kitchen floor in three strides and through the swinging door so hard I thought it was going to shatter when it hit the wall.

Luke grabbed Marilyn Hanson by the back of the neck with one hand and threw him across the room, onto the pressboard coffee table. Two of the legs folded under and dropped him like the world's shittiest playground slide. Marilyn Hanson scrambled up onto all fours, pissing and moaning about his ribs. I took a couple of good steps and punted them just to hear him scream, handing Luke the butcher knife. Handle-first, of course. Safety is everyone's concern. Except for that little fuckhead on the floor. He was a done deal no matter what.

My kick had flopped him down on his belly again, driven the point of his chin into the top of the broken table and sent his teeth through the end of his tongue. He let out one of those big, bawling sobs, the kind where his eyelashes were all clumped together, there wasn't any sound until almost the end of it, and there were strings of slobber that stretched from the top of his open mouth to the bottom like thin crystal floss. His were kind of pinkish, what with the blood and all. The whole bottom of his mouth was full of it, thickened and bubbly with his spit and slopping over his busted bottom lip like soup out of a cracked cup. The front quarter-inch of his tongue came out in the first wave and slid down the tabletop, getting lost among the ashtray debris, bottle caps, and the seeds and stems somebody had picked out of their pot. Part of me wanted to remind myself to find it later, if there was time. I doubted I would remember. I couldn't think of anything really interesting to do with it anyway, besides washing it off and sticking it up my ass and walking around like that for a week or so, and that was never going to happen. I mean, the symbolism was fucking incredible, but the whole reality of it was just way too gay for me to be comfortable with it on a practical level. Plus, although I've never seen it done exactly that way in the movies, sticking a dead guy's tongue up your ass seemed like a good way to end up a zombie of some kind, which I've always saved in the back of my mind for a romantic last resort.

The Raging Whores were stone dead, did I say that yet? Rachel had done both of them. Our little girl was growing up. She was sitting on the arm of the couch watching us, catching her breath. The Raging Whores were watching us too, I guess. I don't know if they knew it or not. They were all tangled up on the couch. One of them had sick candy-pink little kid nipples with thin hoops through them that looked more like aluminum thread than jewelry, but they were sitting on top of tits that were round and tight looking.

"You missed it," Rachel said. "These two were all over each other."

"No way," I groaned.

She smirked at me. The bitch. "Would I lie about something like that?"

Marilyn Hanson howled again. I wanted to cut his throat but I'd already given Lucas the knife. "Goddamn it!" I said. "This asshole gets into stuff like that cause he won't shut up about how great I am, and me, the guy who's so fucking great he can hardly stand himself, I have to kill them before they'll sleep with me. Where's the justice in that?"

Marilyn Hanson was trying to crawl away, the hard-on. Like we were all so busy listening to me talk that we were gonna forget he was crawling around our shoes like a big loud bloody cockroach. I booted him in the side again, and he let out a high-pitched, whining kind of bark, but he more or less quit crying. "I am so pissed off at you right now, you wouldn't even believe it," I told him.

"*Doan kih meh!*" he said. "*You guyth ah lie mah heroth oh tum-theh! Doan kih meh!*"

"Jesus Christ," I said. "That's it, that's the one. If we're gonna rate the most pathetic fucking thing we've ever heard, this guy's got my vote."

Rachel was stabbing the arm of the couch between her thighs, waiting for something to happen. She crinkled up her nose. "What is that smell?" she said, and was going to cover her face with her hand, but then she realized her glove was all covered in blood and thought better of it.

"Wonderboy shit himself," Lucas smirked.

"If that's not hero worship in the 21st century I don't know what is," I told them. "*'I love you! I love you!* Now smell my filthy excrement.'"

"That is *bad*," Rachel said, turning her head and trying to find a direction that would get her nose out of the line of fire. "And they're gonna find him like that, with his pants all full of poop."

"I'm pretty sure that's the last thing they're gonna be worried about," I said, and Marilyn Hanson saw what was coming and started bawling again, so I couldn't hear for sure, but I think Lucas might have actually laughed at that.

58

Rachel

Dave and I went ripping through the house to make sure there wasn't anybody else around, and when we came back downstairs, it was done. Marilyn Hanson was slumped with his back against a dingy white wall, throat cut, entrails in his lap. Lucas had ripped down most of the pin-ups and rock magazine pages and serial killer photos and replaced them with one big, sprawling, bloody word, in letters about a foot high.

AWESOME.

"Impressive," Dave said. He shook a Kool into his mouth from a pack he'd found somewhere and leaned over to light it on a candle, one of those lame ones that look like a human hand and then start bleeding red wax when they burn down a little bit. Total Spencer Gifts-sheik. "Reminds me of the early-Manson renaissance period of the late 60's, although I'm not sure there's enough evidence to support your deviation from the traditional form. The juxtaposition of blood and old white paint is daring, a fair example of stark minimalism."

He stopped and gave me one of those looks that mean either he's gone around the bend and won't be back for a while or he's just pulling my leg. "This man could be the Warhol of his generation."

I nodded at our number one fan. "I hope this doesn't make him some kind of martyr."

"An obscure underground legend, perhaps, but I doubt he's got what it takes to be a martyr."

"He didn't have what it took to be a singer either, but that didn't stop him," Lucas said.

We stood there, watching the blood dry. There's a shade between new red and old brown that's pretty, from a certain angle in a certain light. "It seems to me that maybe you guys just got into this so you could stand around and be wiseasses after you did it," I said.

"It wasn't the only reason, but it sure didn't hurt anything," Dave nodded, staring at the two skanks I'd taken care of all by my lonesome. "Plus, I like blue tits."

"It's better than culinary school," Lucas offered.

"Although," Dave said, gesturing pointedly with his cigarette, "it could be construed as preparing a banquet for an army of maggots."

"Sick!" I said.

"I know," Dave sighed. "No matter what you do in life, it's always like going to cooking school." He flicked ash on either a large or small intestine and looked at us. "We should get out of here."

I was ready to go anywhere that didn't smell like poop. "Homework?" I asked him.

"The Wonder Years is gonna be on."

"Don't you wanna, *you know,* with the bimbos?" I said. "They're kind of attractive, if you're into that trashy whore look."

"Which I am. But this kid reeks. Besides, Eddie Pinetti is gonna kick the crap out of Kevin tonight."

He and Lucas looked at each other for a second and then they took off, Lucas making the back door first because

Dave paused at the last second to keep from becoming part of the door jamb. I dropped my knife and followed as fast as I could. I caught up with them three blocks away, but they let me. The softies.

I was glad it was dark. They couldn't see my eyes water.

59

Rachel

For the rest of the weekend and the next few days we didn't do much but sit around the house and watch the news. Dave had stopped going to class altogether as far as I could tell, and neither of us ever really knew what Lucas did. Sometimes he was there and sometimes he wasn't. We never knew if he was going to classes or not, because when he left the house he never took anything with him but a Mountain Dew or a beer and a black ink pen--one of those with a dark gray tube and a black rounded cap, because apparently he refused to use any other kind.

Sometimes he would go to the university library when it opened at 7:00am and disappear into the stacks with a pair of earplugs and a list of books, and he wouldn't come out until they shut down for the night at 11:30. Dave told me this in one of his rare sharing moods. He would never tell me very much about Lucas, even if I asked him directly. It was hard to pin Dave down on anything if he didn't want to be pinned; he'd start making fun of something you said or make up some asinine reason why you would need an answer for something, and before you knew it you were so busy bantering and trying to keep up with him that you forgot what you'd asked. Once I'd figured that trick out and tried to stop him, he'd say "Hey bitch, if you're not gonna be interesting or entertaining in any way, why don't you go lay under my bed with my fucking textbooks where you belong?"

It's hard to argue with that.

The weather had turned weird on us for the end of October--warm, sunny days and crisp, breezy nights. During the day you wanted ice cream; at night you wanted a hoodie and some hot chocolate. It was strange, but I liked it. It was as if for some reason whoever runs the weather had decided to give us all the good stuff at once.

I was lying on Lucas' bed doing my Oceanography homework, which amused Dave to no end, since we were in Illinois and nowhere near an ocean of any kind. It was ridiculous if you thought about it. But I didn't want to think about it, I just wanted the three Science credits it was worth.

Dave and Lucas were sitting on the floor, playing a seemingly endless tournament of Mortal Kombat II on Peter's old Super Nintendo. I think they were less interested in the game than they were in another opportunity to talk shit to each other. Dave did most of the talking, of course, between handfuls of this completely nasty popcorn that he'd found in a big tin Christmas bucket in the back of Peter's closet. The bucket was divided down the center, half chocolate, half cheese, and all stale. It even *smelled* stale. And he was just wolfing it down, chasing it with slugs from a six-pack of Killian's Red.

Lucas had taken his usual route to nourishment, a handful of pills from his Ziploc freezer bag and big plastic Hardee's cup that held some noxious mixture of Mountain Dew, ice cubes, and a grim amount of clear alcohol of one variety or another. He ate that one handful of pills like Dave ate popcorn, shaking them into his mouth through the top of his fist and crunching them with his teeth. The only difference was that he would occasionally snap his head from side to side as they started to kick in.

"Yeah!" Dave cried. "How does it feel to get your ass kicked, hot shot? Hurts, doesn't it?" He worked a combination on his controller that ripped Lucas' fighter's head off. *"Feel it feel it feel it!"*

He dropped the controller and threw his fists in the air. "Yes! You lose!"

"You're really mature," I muttered.

"Shut up and do your homework," he said. "One of us better get a degree in something, or we're all gonna starve to death."

I put my finger down to mark my place in *The Ocean and You* and looked up at him. "So why don't you do it?"

He smirked and reached for his beer. "Hey, it's too late for me. You're the one who kept going to class and taking notes and all that crap. Now you gotta live with it."

Lucas smiled to himself, his thumbs flying across the buttons on his controller with a sound like a muffled typewriter. Dave howled and lunged for his own controller, trying to recover.

"What the fuck, you cheater!" he said. "This round doesn't count. Unless I win. Then it counts."

"Snooze you lose," Lucas told him, his one-sided smile glowing blue in the light from the television.

"Fuck! Fuck! Goddamn it you asshole!" Dave yelled. "What the--at least let me hit you a couple of--*fuck! Die you piece of shit! Die die die!*"

Lucas dropped his controller as his character turned Dave's into a baby in a diaper. "Game over. I win."

"This isn't over, LaRusso," Dave said, doing his best to sound threatening. "This is a *long way* from over."

"Do you know any references that aren't from TV?" I asked him. I shut my book. I knew I wouldn't be back to it for a while.

Dave tipped his beer bottle in my direction. "Fuck you, Rasputin. How's that?"

"Brilliant. By the way, have either of you decided what to do about your classes?"

"What's wrong with them?" Lucas said.

"I thought you said you were failing."

Lucas, still sitting in a black vinyl beanbag chair on the floor, reached up into the assorted odds and ends on his desk and somehow pulled out the remote control to Pete's stereo, which he'd claimed along with the room. "I said fuck grades. I never said I was failing." He pressed a button and thumbed the volume down to a pleasant level. You wouldn't think there was any such thing as a pleasant level for the Revolting Cocks' *Linger Ficken' Good* album, but there is.

"I'd pretty much decided to follow a predetermined course of events and fail miserably," Dave said. He switched over to one-player mode and started punching buttons again.

"That's courageous," I said.

"What can I say? I'm a victim of circumstances beyond the scope of my ability, much like Napoleon at Waterloo, or General George Armstrong Custer at Little Bighorn."

"I think I liked you better when you stuck to the TV references," I told him. "At least then you sounded less pretentious."

He shot lightning at the other guy on the screen and snickered to himself. "What are we gonna do today, anyway?"

"If there was a segue there, I missed it completely," I said.

"You can't segue from crap to brilliance. It just doesn't work."

"Thanks a lot," I said, and looked at Lucas. "What do you want to do?"

"Well," Dave turned his head toward me slightly, never taking his eyes off the screen, "I thought maybe I'd open up the blinds, let some sunshine in, clean the place up, make up four weeks of Art Education assignments I haven't done, and cook us a five-course meal with all the trimmings. After that, I'd take a shower, do my laundry, and kill somebody."

Lucas took a few hearty swallows from his 90-proof Mountain Dew concoction and watched Dave kicking ass. "Sounds like a lot of work."

Dave leaned back like he was trying to land a big game fish and clicked buttons. "You're right. I have to budget my time wisely. Let's skip all that other crap and just go kill some assholes."

"You're studying to be an art teacher?" I laughed.

He shot me an irritated look. "If you want to be a pedophile, being an art teacher is the perfect job."

"Everyone thinks art teachers fuck cocker spaniels," Lucas said.

Dave nodded. "Plus you get your own little 'supply closet,' if you know what I mean."

"And," Lucas said, lighting a cigarette, "you can always spill paint on some kid's crotch and wipe it off for a half hour."

Dave's jaw dropped; he forgot about punching buttons and his fighter got the crap kicked out of him. "That's really sick," he said. "I don't know whether to be horrified or shake your hand."

"I'm not shaking with you," Lucas told him. "If I do that, it's more or less saying that someday I'll be touching the crotches of third graders second-hand."

"You'd prefer first-hand?" I said.

"No," Dave said. "You use the first hand to cover their mouth so no one hears them cry."

"This is the sickest conversation I've ever heard," I told them, and started stuffing my books into my bag.

Dave snorted. "Yeah, but you don't get out all that much."

I picked up the other controller and Dave took it easy on

me for a few rounds until I figured out what I was doing. After that he'd let me almost kill him every round and then come back at the end and humiliate me. It was more fun than it sounds. I'm not one of those people who always has to win at stupid little crap. Besides, I liked listening to Dave talk shit when he won, which he did, every time.

I don't know how long we went on like that, but at some point Lucas finished his drink, stood up, took a ream of paper off the desk, and walked out. Without a word, as usual.

"Where's he going?" I said.

Dave's guy finished beating mine into a standing coma, then handed him a string of paper dolls by using some code he wouldn't teach me. "His term paper's due today," he said.

"*That* was a term paper?" I said.

Dave dropped his controller and stretched until something popped. "He's got some English Lit class, the professor's a real hard-on. He told them on the first day that the only way they could pass the class was to show up every day and take a shitload of notes, or write a 300-page paper comparing six novels written before 1850 by guys named John. He was probably just trying to be a smartass, but it was in the syllabus and everything."

My brain cringed. "Why the hell would Lucas write the paper?" I said. "That's insane."

Dave shrugged. "It was an 8:00 class. And fuck that guy. Besides, it only took him like three weeks."

The whole concept of it was madness. All that work,

just to avoid getting up early and to give a big, resounding FUCK YOU to a guy you'd decided deserved one a few minutes after meeting him for the first time. In its way it was admirable, even awe-inspiring. But it was so crazy and pointless and tragic that I wanted to scream and cry and pull my hair out just thinking about it.

I looked at Dave. "Did you ever stop to think about what you guys could accomplish if you ever put even a minimum effort into doing things the way you're supposed to? Like going to class and doing homework and all that?"

He yawned. "I'm not really into accomplishment."

"You don't want to be good at anything?"

"One time I read this story in some book Lucas had lying around. It was about some guy who had lied about his brother all the time when they were kids, and then the brother died and the lying asshole felt bad about it. The story was okay, I guess. But the last line was kick-ass. I read it like 100 times, even wrote it out and carried it around in my wallet."

"What was it?" I asked.

He took out his duct tape wallet and poked through scraps of paper that held the names of CDs he wanted to buy, movies he meant to rent, books he would read if he could find them, phone numbers and addresses until he found a receipt with one sentence scrawled on it in blue ink:

It is not worth becoming what there is left for you to become.

60

<u>Dave</u>

Usually you couldn't sell any textbooks back until like the last week of a semester, but since kids were running away from school like it was a bully with dog crap on his hand, they changed the rules and you could do it anytime. That seemed to me like they might be taking that whole helpful-and-understanding thing a little too far. But nobody from the university administration had asked for my opinion, so I decided to take advantage of it.

Most of the time I couldn't even convince those assholes that I was actually attending their school, or that I had actually earned credits. I spent a lot of time at the end of every semester going around to teachers who barely remembered me, convincing them to sign papers that vouched for my existence and my participation in their classes, and having meetings with the ombudsman. I can never remember what an ombudsman is.

It might be Greek for "jackass with an easy, high-paying job who can't remember your name," but don't quote me on that.

Since I had two sets of books to sell back, mine and Petey the Pirate's, I had to split them up into two groups to avoid suspicion. I took Pete's back first. Mine were just as useless, but I was still hoping to think of a way out of the crash landing I knew my GPA was about to take. If worse came to worse I could always go to Lucas, who never has any trouble thinking up a plan to stick it to the Man.

I had actually asked Luke if he wanted half the money I

was going to get from Pete's books, but he told me to keep it all. He said it was a good idea and I deserved the full compensation for it. So we dug all the stuff out, threw it in a backpack, and trucked it over to the student union, where we were supposed to meet Rachel after some meeting she was having with her Biology professor to do some serious grade-grubbing.

I had to stand in line for like a half hour, but I finally got away with an empty backpack and $134.07. Not too shabby. Especially since I hadn't actually done anything to earn it. I don't care what anybody's dad says, free money is always the best kind.

The plan was that I would meet Mr. and Mrs. Psycho at Burger King, and then we'd take off for somewhere else. Preferably the record store and McDonalds, because whatever chemicals they spray on crap at Burger King to make it taste flame-broiled always make me sick for like an hour after I eat it, and there's no good reason to put up with that if you actually have money.

Burger King was crowded, but it wasn't hard to find Lucas. I just looked where everybody else was looking.

Those two cops, Reisman and Frenchie the Fridge, were making a big deal out of trying to throw some kind of scare into my man Luke. They loomed over him on either side, grinning. I pulled Pete's Misfits stocking cap out of the backpack, put it on, and sat down at a table full of kids too wrapped up in being nosy to be pissed off about me invading their space.

"I'm surprised to see you around," Reisman was saying.

"I figured you would have packed up and left town."

Lucas, of course, just looked at him. And not that nervous, blinking, oh-god-I-wish-this-guy-would-just-go-away kind of look, either. He just looked bored.

"Oh that's right," Reisman grinned, and smoothed his tie down. Big tie-smoother, that guy. "You're the quiet one. Where's your buddy with the big mouth?"

There's a definite irony when a hot-shit investigator asks where you are and you're sitting five feet behind him, drinking somebody else's Mello Yello. Frenchie the Fridge, who didn't look like the kind of guy who would recognize irony or appreciate it if you pointed it out to him, poked Lucas in the shoulder. "He's talking to you, stupid."

A little one-sided grin spread across Lucas' face and he turned his eyes to the Fridge. He said nothing. It was almost too much to take. Kind of like the anticipation of watching some kid you hate shoot a roman candle at a shed full of dynamite.

"If he doesn't have anything to say here, maybe we ought to take him back to the station and ask him again," Reisman said. "What do you think?"

Frenchie put on a big grin for show and stretched. "Suits me," he said. "I don't have anywhere to be for the rest of the afternoon."

He reached over and shoved at Lucas again. "What do you think about that, fat boy?"

Fat boy. He actually called Lucas *fat boy.* Like some bullshit jocko-homo high school bully. It made me want to kill him bad.

"I think," Lucas said, "you should stop touching me."

Frenchie the Fridge poked him again. "Oh yeah? Well let's just say, for giggles, that I don't want to stop. What then, fat boy?"

I actually saw Rachel wince as Lucas' grin spread to both corners of his mouth. "Then I make you stop."

"Threatening a police officer," Reisman said. "Not a good idea, my man."

Lucas grinned. "Insult me, lay your hands on me in an aggressive way, and then hide behind your badge when I offer to defend myself," he said, staring at the Fridge. "You chickenshit motherfucker. You wouldn't make a pimple on a real cop's ass."

Holy fucking Lola.

Did you ever hear 35-40 people suck in breath at the same time? It sends a shiver up your back, no kidding. And the next thought that runs through your head is *come on come on come on*, because even though you know that something is going to happen, and quick, it's never soon enough. That's a small thing, I know, but it's part of what makes life worth living, for sure.

Frenchie the Fridge went apeshit. Reisman caught him in mid-lunge and drove him back, pushing him like one of those blocking sleds I've seen football players use. By the time he got the Fridge out of hitting distance and calm, Reisman's tie was wrinkled and crispy strands of his hair were hanging around the sides of his face, which was red with the effort. He kept saying "Not here, not here," and that sure didn't help their public image any. The kids I was sitting with were actually sharp enough to wonder, aloud, where round 2 was going to go down.

I had to admit, it was a good question.

Lucas hadn't moved. He was still slouched in his chair, grinning. He looked at me and winked. Since I didn't see how he could have known where I was, or if I was there at all, that was pretty fucked up, right there.

It seemed to suddenly dawn on the pigs that there were a lot of people watching them. Or at least it started to bother them when they realized that they looked like assholes.

"Nice talking to you," Reisman puffed, trying to get his breath back and his hair back together. The smile on his face was so forced it was painful to look at. "We'll have to do it again some time."

Lucas' grin was back to one side of his mouth again. Reisman waited for him to say something for a beat too long and walked out of the Burger King dining room with one hand in the small of Frenchie the Fridge's back, guiding him like a prom date. It sort of made sense. I had a feeling somebody was going to get fucked before the night was over.

Luke said something to Rachel that I couldn't hear and went out the back way. I caught up with her by the information desk.

"Where'd he go?" I said.

She made a face. "He said he had some errands to run, and that you and I should stick together. He's going to catch up with us later."

We headed for the house, neither one of us saying

anything. "I don't care if it does make me sound like a wuss," she finally blurted out. "I've got a really bad feeling about this."

"Yeah," I told her. "We can go to the wuss meetings together, cause I don't feel too hot about it either."

61

<u>Rachel</u>

The day was too nice to go to my afternoon classes, and Dave couldn't remember if he even had any classes that day, so we ended up in front of the television. We watched an episode of *Tales From the Darkside*, which made Dave flip his lid because it had been written by Stephen King. Then we watched *Saved By the Bell* a couple of times, and Tom and Jerry cartoons, and *Thundercats*. He made the usual Dave-watching-TV conversation, cross-referencing everything until my brain was in serious danger of shutting down from a pop-culture overload.

"Can I ask you something and have you be serious?" I said during one of the commercials.

He tilted his head to one side and looked at me in a series of sidelong blinks, the way he does when he knows something vaguely unpleasant is coming. "Maybe."

"I mean it. No jokes."

He picked up his acoustic guitar and strummed it once, muting the strings with the side of his palm, making an adjustment to the tuning keys, and strumming it softly again with the side of his thumb. "I'll give it a shot."

I gave myself a moment, to see if he was going to look at me and to make sure I wanted to go through with it. The answers were no and no, but I pressed on. "Is it not totally obvious at this point that I like Lucas?" I said.

He sniffed, strummed three soft, pretty chords that sounded vaguely familiar, and looked up at me. "You're not walking around with little cartoon hearts coming out of your eyes or anything. But yeah."

"So you know."

"Yeah."

There was a pause. "Does *he* know?" I asked.

Dave gave me another sidelong, stuttering look and plucked strings. "I said something to him about it once. He's aware of the theory."

It's such an odd way to put it. *Aware of the theory.* What did that mean? That Lucas didn't believe it? That he knew but didn't care? That Dave had made some sort of joke out of it and Lucas had taken it at face value? *He's aware of the theory.* There was so much that was so wrong with it, so much that left me hanging in the middle and worse off than I was before.

"Then what's the problem?" I said. I tried to sound low-key and casual. I doubt it worked.

Dave frowned slightly, and I could tell he wasn't trying to be an ass. "The problem being...?"

"He's not interested in girls in general, or just me?"

Dave shrugged. "The subject never came up. I don't think he's gay, though."

"He doesn't find me attractive?"

"Never said anything one way or another."

"Because I'm pregnant?" I said. I was starting to sound desperate, but I didn't care. How often can you get Dave to put both feet on solid ground and converse like a normal human being? I wanted some sort of revelation on this subject before his tether broke and he floated away into the stratosphere. "Come on, you guys never talk about girls at all?"

"We've got better crap to make jokes about than that," he smirked. He found a guitar pick in his pocket, put it in his mouth, and began rummaging through the junk on the end table for a pack of cigarettes.

I checked to make sure the windows were open. Lucas had been soaking something in a plastic trashcan full of gasoline for about a week and a half, and the fumes were starting to get persistent. "I don't get it," I said. "I've done everything but get naked and write DO ME on my stomach. I even rubbed up against him and told him we could--"

Dave stared at me.

"Well, you know. I said it kind of like I was joking, but still."

He found a cigarette in one of Lucas' old packs and lit it. "Yeah, he doesn't like to be touched."

"Even by girls?" I said.

"By anybody."

"Great," I said. "Once in my life I have a wild animal attraction for a guy and he doesn't like to be touched."

The tobacco crackled as Dave inhaled, and he blew out a thin cloud. "I don't profess to understand the first thing about what chicks like, but you're fucked up."

"What's that supposed to mean?"

Dave grinned. "He never says anything, he dresses like a wino, and his idea of a fun evening is busting through the front door of a house and killing everybody inside. You don't have a wild animal attraction, you're attracted to a wild animal."

"Oh *that's* nice," I said, though he did have a point.

"Hey, he's better than I am," Dave said. "You're cute and everything, but I wouldn't bang you till your heart stopped beating."

I looked at him closely, trying to see if he was kidding. "You'd really do that to me?" I asked.

He put the guitar down with exaggerated caution and leapt out of Lucas' chair, clapping his hands together like a Little League coach. "Who wants ice cream?"

62

Dave

What I like to do when eating ice cream is get a decent sugar cone and three scoops, all of them as far apart on the flavor spectrum as it's possible to get. I've experimented with more than three, but it gets messy. I'm not a big fan of licking anything off my fingers unless I absolutely have to, and I tend to wear khaki's a lot, and since there aren't a lot of ice cream flavors that blend well with tan, you can see the problem. I think that day, working down from the top, I was eating Bubblegum, Peanut Butter Chocolate, and

Coconut Almond. All of which were delicious.

"This is some good ice cream," I said, when I'd gotten comfortable enough with my licking pattern to make conversation a non-effort. We were walking, of course. Rachel had a license and no car, and I have no desire to ever drive a car in my life because it seems like a pain in the ass and I've always found it more interesting to bum rides off other people.

"I'm not even going to ask where you got the money to pay for it," Rachel said, referring to the ice cream, for those of you following along at home who may be a little slow on the uptake.

"I sold Pete's books back," I said. Apparently Lucas hadn't bothered to tell her why we were going to the student union, which made me wonder why she'd tagged along in the first place. "Nobody else called dibs."

She was having Mint Chocolate Chip and Rainbow Sherbet, both of which I considered to be secondary, perhaps even tertiary flavors, although I did find the combination to be interesting. After a few licks to mix the colors, I had to admit it did make a strange presentation. I thought about asking for a taste, to see what the flavor and texture were like, but I didn't really feel comfortable with that.

"Hey," I said. "Did I ever tell you about the time Lucas got into a fight at Baskin Robbins?"

That made her laugh really hard for some reason, and she stuck her nose right into the Sherbet. After that I was positive I wasn't going to ask for a taste.

"No," she said, wiping at the tip of her nose with a paper napkin. "But I would love to hear it."

The story, basically, is that for a while, whenever we had the money, Pete and Lucas and I would go to Baskin Robbins and work on sampling all 31 flavors. But we couldn't ever do anything the easy way, so you didn't get to pick what you were going to eat. Everybody got a two-scoop cone. For instance, if it was my cone, Pete would pick one flavor and Lucas would pick the other one, and then I'd have to eat it, whether I liked it or not. It sounds goofy, but we found a lot of good combinations that way. And it was another opportunity to be a dick to your friends, which we were always on the lookout for.

Anyway, one time Lucas had gotten a combo that he really liked. I can't remember what it was, but Pete and I were fucking with him, trying to make it the worst thing possible. Blueberry Cheesecake and Black Walnut maybe, because we knew he hated blueberries and walnuts. But then he said it was good, and you can never tell if Lucas is lying or not, so we both wanted to try it. He just held it out and let us each take a lick, because we aren't squeamish about stuff like that.

Apparently, a lot of people *are* squeamish about stuff like that. In the eyes of some people, like the redneck townies who were sitting at tables with their girlfriends, Lucas might as well have pulled out his dick and let us each take a lick of that instead. Admittedly, it probably didn't help that Lucas and Pete had painted fingernails, or that Pete had green hair, or that I had fire engine red hair, or that

Pete was wearing mascara and his cut-off pirate pants and Halloween socks.

One of the rednecks said "Fucking *faggots*," and his friends all snickered.

Pete could do a good gay lisp. Not as good as Lucas, but a lot better than me. "I swear to *God*," he said, just a little too loud. "If they made cock-flavored ice cream, I would be *soooo* fat. Especially if it was *chocolate* cock-flavored ice cream. There's nothing in the world I like better than the taste of a big, chocolate cock."

The whole place froze up. He'd managed to hit the Townie Two--racism and homophobia--in one shot. Pete wasn't a non-stop clever kind of guy, but he definitely had his moments. Anyway, the biggest redneck, who you could tell was gonna be one of those guys with a huge gut and suspenders in like ten years, opened his big yap to say something and Lucas slammed his ice cream cone right into the redneck's face. I mean *hard*. The ice cream smashed all over his big dumb face, the cone broke, and bloody ice cream goop sprayed out everywhere. Lucas had broken his nose, busted his top lip, and broken off three of his teeth. Then he just stood there with one of those half-smiles on his face, giving the redneck the old snake eye.

That was the first time either Pete or I had seen the snake eye, or somebody snap like that, or somebody get their teeth knocked out. It was scary. I felt like my skeleton was made of thick copper wire and somebody had hooked me up to a light socket. My brain was taking everything in, but it wasn't making any decisions. I was aware that ice cream was dripping all over my hand and the top of my shoe, and I just let it. Pete said later that he felt the same way, only he was still licking his ice cream, because he was kind of a little bitch about stuff like keeping his shoes looking new and clean all the time.

The redneck hit the tile floor on his ass and let out a big *ooof.* Lucas looked at the other rednecks and their dates. Two guys, three girls.

"Anybody else got something to say?" he asked.

Nobody did. They didn't have anything to look at either. They just knew they didn't want to look at him, or me, or Pete. The fat redneck coughed and more blood came out of his mouth, and he spit his teeth out into his lap. I know there were three, because I counted them. For some reason I had an incredible urge to pick them up and put them in my pocket and run, just so I could stare at them later in the palm of my hand. I was wound up so tight--it was like being really horny, only it had nothing to do with my wiener for once.

There was some Goth kid working the counter--dyed black hair, pasty skin, eyebrow ring, the whole deal. You could look at him and tell that he hated his job, that every day he had to deal with stupid rednecks coming in and making their idiot comments just loud enough for him to hear. He was keeping a straight face, but his eyes were grinning from ear to ear.

Lucas pulled out a $20 and dropped it on the counter in front of him. It doesn't sound like much, but to us $20 is a lot of money. "Sorry about the mess," he said.

The corners of the goth kid's mouth twitched. "No problem," he said.

"What do I look like?" Lucas asked him.

The kid took the $20 and put it in his pocket. "I've been here since 4:00," he said. "I haven't seen you yet."

And we left, just like that. No cops, no nothing. We just walked away unharmed, unless you count the ice cream on my shoe.

Rachel looked at me and licked her ice cream. "And that was before... uh... *other* activities?"

"Yeah," I said. "Yeah. A little bit. For me and Pete anyway."

"What about the big guy?"

"Him too, I think," I nodded. There was something I liked about her calling him *the big guy,* but I didn't know what it was. I would never call Lucas *the big guy,* sort of the same way I would never call a black person *nigger,* even though I really like that word for the way it sounds, how it feels coming out of your mouth and the instant shitstorm it always stirs up when it comes out of a melanin-deprived face like mine. But *the big guy* sounded good when she said it, and it kind of made me feel loopy inside.

"You never asked him?" she frowned. "I know more about my worst enemies than you know about your best friends, you know that?"

I shrugged and licked ice cream.

"It's sick and sad if you think about it."

"Yeah," I said, pronouncing it *yuh* the way Lucas does, which made us both laugh. "On my personal list of sick and sad shit, that ranks right up there."

And then came the whistling, and that's when everything got totally fucked up.

63

<u>Rachel</u>

"Oh Jesus," I said. Louder than I should have, maybe, but I don't know if they heard it. If they did I don't think it made any difference. Jesus didn't seem to hear it either, for that matter. Though if he had, I doubt we were a priority case in his In-basket.

We fucked up because we weren't paying attention to where we were going and what was around us. Nice day, the ice cream, Dave's story, all that. Our heads were up our asses, to coin a Lucas phrase. We had wandered right into the outskirts of Little Greece, where the low-rent frats have their main houses and the rich ones keep their satellite places. These weren't the well-tended, manicured lawns and fresh white paint places--these were the dumps.

Think *Animal House*. Then replace those loveable rebel scamps with rednecks, date rapists, coke dealers, career alcoholics and third-string jocks.

There were five of them sitting on a sagging porch, already pounding them down at 2:30 on a Wednesday afternoon. One of them whistled at me, and that's all it took. The rest of them picked it up and ran with it, trying to impress each other with just how vulgar and "witty" they could be. I heard most of what they said. I won't repeat it.

"Always good to see tomorrow's leaders in their formative years, isn't it?" Dave said, but he never missed a step. It seemed stupid to hurry past them, or cross the street, or turn around and run. You flee if someone's chasing you. If no one is and you take off, somebody just might.

"Shouldn't they be playing volleyball and trying to spike each other in the face?" I said.

Dave bit into the top of his cone and sucked out ice cream like marrow from a leg bone. "Probably shoved the ball up a Computer Science major's ass and passed out before they decided whose turn it was to get it back."

"Only faggots eat ice cream!" one of the frat rats yelled. A skinny, Guido-looking piece of shit in a wifebeater with a gold chain and crucifix around his neck. His buddies hooted and cheered.

Dave looked at me with one eyebrow up and shook his head. "Only faggots know that secret!" he yelled back, which made me laugh.

Guido threw his Bud Light can with a dramatic flourish and charged down porch steps. His buddies were quick to follow. "What'd you say?"

"Oh, shit," Dave muttered. I couldn't tell if he was scared or just amusing himself, as he is prone to do.

"Kick his pansy ass!" another one said, a beefy guy in a Green Bay sweatshirt with the sleeves ripped off and the collar slashed down the front. "He looks like Elvis Costello!"

"I fucking *hate* Elvis Costello," Guido said to no one in

particular.

"Come on, fuck off," I said. "This is stupid."

Guido's open hand shot out and planted itself in Dave's chest, sending him back a couple of steps. I was surprised he didn't fall down. Dave is not known for his physical grace. "Your bitch has got a mouth on her, Elvis. You gonna back that shit up?"

Dave grinned at him. "Hey, you want some of my ice cream?"

"Fuck no I don't want your fucking ice cream, you fucking faggot," Guido said. (Guido *fucking* said?) "Ice cream's for faggots."

I knew then that we were in shit up to our necks. I *knew* it. Dave had that look in his eye, and once he gets on that track, he can't get off it. It's what he has. You may be bigger, or stronger, or have more power or authority. You may be able to do anything you want to him. But he will talk shit to you before, while, and after you do it, because in his mind there is nothing worse than taking abuse with your head down and your mouth shut.

"You sure?" Dave said, and took another lick. "It's a new flavor, you'll like it."

"What flavor?" Green Bay snorted.

"Drunk, sweaty 16 year-old with a roofie swirl," Dave told him, and took one more lick, letting out a soft groan of sheer ecstasy. "Your sister, I think."

And then he held out what was left of the cone, as if he actually believed that Green Bay would want to try it. I laughed and laughed, not wanting to but so scared I couldn't stop.

The frat rats looked at me, and at Dave, and each other. They were thrown.

Then they jumped Dave, and I was thrown.

64

Dave

I'm not Chuck Norris, okay? And it wouldn't have mattered if I was, because it wasn't a Chuck Norris kind of fight. That always cracks me up, where he'll be in a circle of ninjas or Viet Cong or something, and they'll attack him one or two at a time, three at the most. I asked Lucas one time what he thought would happen if they all got on him at once, because Lucas is the kind of guy who knows crap like that.

"They'd kick the living shit out of him," Lucas said, which made me laugh my ass off, because sometimes hearing Lucas say anything is hilarious.

I don't know about Chuck Norris, but they kicked the living shit out of me, that's for sure. Not literally, but almost. I seriously thought I might drop a pantload when they kicked me in the stomach about 20 times in a row, but then they went to work on the kidneys for a little bit, so I was just concentrating on trying not to whiz myself. Looking back on it, I would have to say that it never really occurred to me that a beating was so scatological.

They were a kicking bunch, I'll give them that. Of course, when you fall down on the ground and curl up in a ball to protect yourself, it's not like they're gonna keep bending over to punch you, I guess. What can I say? I'm not a fighter. I tried to get Lucas to teach me once, because I thought it might come in handy some day to be able to kick ass and take names. Lucas tagged me one on the nose, not too hard, according to him, and I saw stars for about 20 minutes, and that was the end of my fighting experience.

Some people are born to just take names, I guess.

I'm not sure what they did to Rachel. We don't talk about it. I know that right before my glasses broke I saw her try to pull somebody off me, and that guy threw her belly-first into the back corner of a truck that was parked on the street. She screamed and fell down and kept screaming. When they left us I crawled over to her and she was still screaming and holding her stomach. The crotch of her jeans was soaked with blood and I was dizzy and I puked. The ice cream was still cold on the way up. I found that very odd.

I don't think she ever forgave me for laughing. Later on, when we weren't so close to it, I wanted to try and explain it to her, but I couldn't think of a way good enough to justify bringing the whole thing up again. I laughed. I laughed until I ran out of breath.

All I could think of was what Lucas was going to do when he found out about this, and how I was probably going to miss it.

65

Dave

I didn't realize I had been watching the doors until I saw the Camaro glide into a parking spot and Lucas climb out of it. They were those cool glass doors that whooshed apart when somebody stepped up to them, just like you see on TV. Everything else in the hospital looked like they'd converted it from some 60's elementary school, but those doors had definite style. Lucas had his shades on, of course, and a burning cigarette in his mouth. He dropped the butt on the blacktop and crushed it with his next step.

I was sitting in one of the waiting room chairs with my ribs taped up and twelve stitches in my face. Two of my teeth were loose, but everybody thought they'd tighten up again if I laid off steak and jelly beans for a week or two. One of the nurses felt bad for me and gave me a roll of adhesive tape; I was trying to piece my glasses back together when Lucas came. I wasn't doing too badly either, considering that my eyes were on the door the whole time.

I had called the house an hour before and left a message on the machine telling him where we were and kind of why. I'd expected him sooner and wanted to ask him where the hell he'd been, but I didn't.

"She lost that kid," I said.

He smiled. At first it was just one side of his mouth; then it spread, until the corners of his mouth were back as far as it could go without surgical assistance. I could see all of his teeth, white and perfectly formed, the kind of choppers you could use as a denture mold. Something very,

very bad happened inside him--I could feel it coming off of him in waves for a second, and then it was gone. He shut the outside part of it off and turned it all back in.

"She okay?" he said.

"I don't know. Nobody will tell me anything."

He grinned. "You?"

"I feel like I got hit by the handicapped bus and all the wheelchairs flew through the windshield and hit me in the head," I told him. "We were just walking down the street and these drunk assholes started beating the fuck out of me. One of them threw her up against a truck when she tried to help me."

"Which drunk assholes?"

"It was that farm-kid frat, the one where they're always playing football in the yard," I said. They probably weren't farm kids, but that's what Pete had called them one time, and it made us laugh, so it stuck. "They came off the fucking porch and beat the shit out of me."

Lucas pulled a thin fold of bills from the pocket of his jeans, peeled off a $20 and handed it to me. "Take a cab back to the house when they let her go."

There was only one taxi service in town; it had two cars and ran from the Amtrak station. I'd never ridden in it and didn't know anybody who had. "What are you gonna do?" I asked, but Lucas was already headed for the sliding doors. And once he's moving he doesn't look back.

66

Rachel

We were sitting in the living room with the lights off and the TV on, because we didn't want to be alone, we didn't want to talk, and we sure as hell didn't want to look at each other. *The Simpsons* was on. Dave was drinking chocolate milk through a fun straw. From time to time, usually during commercials, he would go into the bathroom and vomit when the combined taste of milk and blood got to him.

It was like someone had opened a drain in my body I didn't know I had and let all my insides fall out. The baby was gone but I wasn't thinking about it, exactly. I wasn't thinking about anything. I couldn't concentrate and didn't want to. Every time I tried to focus on something for more than two seconds, whatever object appeared in my inner field of vision turned out to be absolutely horrible. I stared at the TV and tried to let my brain die peacefully, but it refused. The things I had to deal with and atone for weren't going to go away until I'd done my time.

The back door creaked open and we both jumped. I could have sworn I heard Dave laugh; when I looked at him his mouth was still, the television reflecting off the lenses of his broken glasses. We waited and listened for footsteps, but there was nothing.

And then Lucas was there, in the kitchen doorway, filling it. Staring at us. Covered in blood from head to toe, his long hair clumped into black, shining tentacles that hung to the center of his chest and back. His goatee and eyebrows were matted with it. His shirts were plastered to him, their color unrecognizable. In the flickering light of the TV, the thighs of his jeans seemed to be coated in used motor oil.

The smell of him turned my stomach. It was a stale, coppery stink that sank into your fillings and made you taste it, mingled with the musky scent of his exertion. He pulled his cigarette box out of his pocket and shook the last Winston Light into his mouth. When he pulled the Bic out of his jeans I wondered if his pockets were full of blood too.

I covered my mouth with my hand and started to cry. Fear and disgust. Futility and loss. For the first time I felt the way I had always suspected I was supposed to but never really did. New wounds were blooming inside me with every blink and breath; old ones were being re-opened and salted for good measure. Deep in the back of my brain I wondered if that was it, if I was really going to just lose it and go insane. It didn't seem impossible anymore.

"Oh my God," I said.

"Holy shit," Dave added, in a tone that was solemn but impressed.

Lucas blew smoke, checked the television, and looked at us. I could see blood on the white paper of his cigarette. "I'm taking a shower and then I'm out of here," he said.

"Where are we going?" Dave said.

"Anywhere but here," Lucas told him. Then he was gone.

Dave stood up, tossing his half-empty glass of chocolate milk onto the carpet. "You going?"

"I don't know," I said. I was trying not to cry and doing

a bad job of it. "I wish I was dead."

He stared at me, and I could see that the concept of wishing yourself dead was totally alien to him. "If you stay here you might not be okay," he said.

"And if I go with you?" I said. "I'll be safe then?"

"Safer than here."

Through the floor we could hear the water running in the downstairs shower. "You've got to be kidding me!" I cried.

"You saw him," Dave said. "Who in your whole stupid life ever cared about you enough to do that for you?"

"I never asked him to do that!"

Dave smirked. "You didn't *have* to ask him, ass."

He went into his room, turned on the light, and started stuffing everything he owned into an army duffel bag. I got up, painfully, and followed him. "I don't have any clothes here," I said.

He glanced at me. "We'll stop by your apartment, steal you new stuff," he said. "Something."

"We don't have any money," I protested.

He stared at me, one of his eyebrows arched toward the ceiling. "This isn't exactly the time to start worrying about the details."

63

Dave

Lucas didn't have much, so it wasn't hard for him to gather up his essentials. I was going through his CD collection, shoving the good ones into one of Pete's old backpacks and throwing the rest like Frisbees, watching the cases break on the walls. I had already gone through his magazines and picked out all the old copies of *Details* and *Spin* I hadn't read yet.

Rachel came shuffling in like the death of the party and stood in the corner by the door, ready to start crying and snotting it up again at any second. I was hoping she'd keep being a pain in the ass and we'd just drop her, because who wants to go on a long car ride with somebody who cries and whines all the time? But it just wasn't in the cards.

"How quick can you be ready?" Lucas asked her.

"I don't know if I'm going," she said.

Things were looking good.

Lucas kept packing. If she was waiting for him to beg her, she should have packed a lunch. Not that I had anything against her. If she wasn't gonna be a pain in the ass, I was all about having her along. It's not like I don't like her or anything. But it's like Lucas says; people are like razors. If they get dull, or just won't cut it anymore, you throw them away.

"I'm scared," she said. "You're not scared?"

Lucas stuffed the last of his socks and underpants into his bag and zipped it up. "You know that garbage can on the front step?" he asked me.

I grabbed a *Details* with Noah Wyle on the cover and shoved it into the backpack. There wasn't room for anything else in there and it weighed about 50 pounds already. "The 30 gallon decongestant?" I said. "What about it?"

"It's full of boots. I've got the laces tied up, they should be dry, so try to only touch those if you can. Throw one or two in every room, down here too." He looked at Rachel. "You, round up anything that will burn. Gin, lighter fluid, nail-polish remover, anything."

"We're gonna torch the place?" I said.

One side of his mouth went up. "You got it."

"Fucking awesome!" I yelled. I'd always wanted to burn a house down, but it had never been convenient. Say what you will about Lucas, being friends with him is a lot like a lifetime membership to the Make-A-Depraved-Wish Foundation.

"I asked you if you were scared," Betty Bring-Down said, like she was trying to get tough with him.

Part of me kind of hoped he would stab her in the throat and leave her, but what he did was better.

"After the shit we've done, we got no right to be scared of anything," he told her, and turned to me. "Throw your bags by the back door. Ten minutes, we're gone."

Now I don't know much about arson, but Lucas' way made a lot of sense to me. He'd been soaking those gold boots we stole from the Q-Goats for a while, so they were totally saturated. Then we took plastic McDonald's cups, dipped gasoline out of the can and threw it around all over the carpet, furniture and walls. This meant a lot of running up and down the stairs, but I was psyched, so it wasn't as bad as it could have been. When we'd dipped enough out of the can that we could lift it, we horsed it through the living room and into the kitchen.

Lucas locked the front door and made sure all the windows were closed. He unplugged the fridge and pulled the stove away from the wall, working on something at the back of it with a crescent wrench.

"I don't want to be a pain in the ass," I told him, "but--"

He stuck the wrench in his back pocket and grinned. "Remote control arson," he said. "Old-school."

He opened the cabinet over the microwave and took two telephones off the top shelf, the one so high that none of us could see into it without standing on a chair. They didn't look special, just old.

"Okay," I said. "Seriously? I might never get to be in on something like this again. You totally need to explain this to me, in detail."

And he did, and it was fucking brilliant. He'd taken the bottoms off the phones, wrapped the bells inside with sandpaper, and attached kitchen matches to the ring hammers. The next time the phones rang, the matches would light, and boom. No more house.

I was ready to give him credit for pure genius, but he told me he got the idea from the movie *Backdraft*, which somehow left me even more impressed. Not only did he get something useful from TV, but he had the sack to admit it. When I do shit like that I just pretend I thought it up and hope nobody busts me on it.

Anyway, he'd unhooked the gas line--which was now spraying propane--from the back of the stove, and unplugged the fridge to keep the condenser from kicking on, possibly sparking, and blowing the whole works before we were ready.

"Depending on how good the city gas lines are, we might take out the whole block," he said.

Holy shit.

He plugged the first phone in and set it on an end table in the living room, with the receiver off the hook. "I'm gonna go down to Pete's room and plug this one in," he said, holding up the other one. "Stay here. When I get back up here, and I'm outside, hang the other one up and run like hell. The door's set to lock. Just slam it behind you and keep running."

"What if somebody calls before I get out the door?" I asked. It wasn't likely, but stranger things have happened.

He grinned at me. "Then you and Pete can catch up on old times," he said. "My advice would be don't think about it, don't slip on your way out, and don't look back."

64

Rachel

I was sitting in the Camaro, waiting for the house to blow up. Then I closed my eyes, and when I opened them again we were in the Walgreens' parking lot, and Dave was saying he felt like he needed 23 showers in a row, and possibly a lobotomy. My eyelids went down again, and the next time they came up the car was easing to a stop on gravel, and there were no streetlights anywhere. Lucas killed the engine and got out.

"Where are we?" I sighed.

Dave leaned up from the backseat. "Beats me," he said. "What's wrong with you? I mean, seriously. Are you gonna die or anything? Cause you should probably tell us if you are. That's just common courtesy."

I tried to swallow and nothing happened. "I feel really, really bad," I told him. "Death might be a pleasant alternative."

"Fuck," he said. He actually sounded concerned, which I found touching.

Lucas reappeared and opened the passenger door. "We're good," he said. He slipped one arm under my knees and the other around my shoulders and lifted me out of the car like I was made of feathers. And then he was carrying me, my whole body floating gently up and down as we climbed wooden stairs. There was an open door ahead of us, but whatever lay beyond it was hidden in total darkness.

"Where are we?" I said, but I was out again before I heard an answer.

65

Dave

That house was the closest thing to a mansion I've ever been in, and I have to admit it was pretty sweet. We tucked Rachel away in the master bedroom and I roamed the place while Lucas brought stuff inside. They had three big-screen TVs, leather furniture, a Jacuzzi, and a kitchen full of appliances that looked like they'd never been touched.

White carpeting. The kind of place you could picture a 70's rockstar living in, like if one of the guys from Pink Floyd had decided he needed a quaint little vacation home in the middle of Bumfuck, Illinois.

Lucas told me at some point who the place belonged to, but I can't remember. It was a summer house for some rich douche bag from Chicago who had gone to our school and apparently managed to make that work for him somehow. I don't know what kind of tasteless asshole could fall in love with Friedman to the point where he would build a huge vacation house on the back side of lovely Lake Suede and spend three or four months a year there by choice.

It takes all kinds, I guess. Fortunately, all kinds leave a lot of non-perishable food in their walk-in pantries and stuff in the freezer, so we weren't going to starve to death any time soon. I was still sort of pissed off that he, Lucas, had obviously been there before, several times, without me, and wondered for about the hundredth what else he did when he vanished for hours on end.

I had been really excited about hitting the road, which seemed like the definite no-turning back point for a life of adventure and excitement--sort of like the modern-day equivalent of joining the crew of a pirate ship. After finding out that the road was only about 12 miles long, I was pretty bummed out.

"This sucks," I told Lucas when I found him on the back deck, looking out over the lake. "I thought we were taking off?"

He handed me his cigarette. "We gotta wait. I'm not

sure what kind of shape she's in."

He was right, but I stood by my original assessment. It still sucked.

"Buck up, little camper," he grinned. "I got something that'll make you feel better."

"Prostitutes?" I said.

"Better than that." He started pulling cell phones out of his pockets and lining them up on the deck railing. I think there were four of them. "Pick one."

I pointed at one of them. "Where'd you get these?"

"They're not gonna need 'em anymore." He took the phone I'd picked and dialed a number. When he started talking, it was in the greatest gay voice I've ever heard in my life. It sounded absolutely nothing like him at all.

"Action 8 news? Is this the hotline?" he said, and I had to clap my hand over my mouth to keep from howling. "Listen, I happen to know that in 10 minutes, the house at 315 North Normal Street in Friedman is going to blow sky-high. Yes I'm serious. No I don't want to tell you how I know, honey. That's right. 315 North Normal Street, Friedman. I know you have people over there, I got the number off of one of your little news vans, sugar. Ten minutes. Don't miss it!"

He hung up and handed me the phone. "Lake?"

I cocked my arm back and whipped it, which did nothing to improve the feeling in my ribs. We held our breath and heard the splash when it hit the water. "Is it wrong that I feel like whistling the theme from *The Andy Griffith Show* right now?" I said.

"Nah," he said. "But we probably ought to see if one of these big-ass TVs is still hooked up to something, or we're gonna miss the fireball."

I guess $65 a month for cable you aren't going to watch isn't too much to pay if you're fucking loaded, because all the TVs were still up and running. We got beers and parked ourselves in front of the biggest one just in time to see Action 8 news break into Must-See-TV. Todd Byrne was fumbling around with his microphone, trying to angle himself so that the wind didn't mess his hair up too badly.

"Think there's any chance he might blow up too?" I said.

Lucas shrugged. "I just hope all that gasoline hasn't dried out too much," he said. "We're running a little behind schedule."

"How much time do we have?" I said. "Because if it's at all possible, we should tape this."

We vaulted off the couch and started rummaging around for blank video tapes. I found some that were labeled *XXX*, but I tossed them aside to watch later. There's no sense in ruining perfectly good porn to watch something blow up unless you absolutely have to.

Lucas found one that said *Guiding Light* on it, which we both thought was pretty funny. He shoved it into the VCR and set it up quick.

"--anonymous call a few moments ago," Byrne was saying. "Police are blocking off the street as we speak, and evacuating nearby residents from their homes. Still no word as to who owns the house, believed to be a rental property, or who might live inside, but--"

"It's almost tempting to not blow it up," I said. "That would be awesome. Just make all of them show up, and cause a big panic, and then nothing."

Lucas tossed me one of the cell phones. "It's time."

"You're gonna let me do it?" I said.

He grinned out of one side of his mouth. "Who's your buddy?"

I wanted to hug that big ugly fucker. Instead, I opened the phone, punched six buttons, put my thumb on the seventh, looked at the TV, and pressed.

And nothing happened.

"Oh what the fuck!" I screamed. "Bullshit! You've gotta be fucking kidding me! There's no way that didn't--"

Boom.

"Probably a delay cause it's live," Lucas said, and took another pull off his beer.

When we blow something up, we *blow something up.*

If a crack opened up in the earth and hell erupted out of it, it would probably look only slightly cooler than our house did right then. It knocked the cameraman on his ass, but he kept it pointed in the right direction so only the angle changed. The blast was so loud that it fucked up the microphones they were using, and everything started buzzing and screeching. Todd Byrne was yelling something, crawling toward the camera on all fours with flaming shit falling out of the sky on him. The back of his Action 8 windbreaker was smoking, but he basically looked okay.

You don't get it all in one lifetime, I guess.

The pine trees in front of the house were on fire, the yard was on fire, and when the camera pulled back a little more, you could see that the houses on either side of ours were going up too. It didn't take long for the fire department to show up and start hosing it all down, for all the good that did. Talk about pissing on a forest fire.

"You know what?" I said. "We've done a lot of really bad shit, but this feels like it might be the worst thing ever."

Lucas lit a cigarette. "How so?"

"I'm not sure," I said. "It's like, okay, we kill a bunch of assholes, and that doesn't bother me, so why do I feel weird about blowing up a bunch of houses and shit?"

"It's different," he shrugged. "You saying you don't like it?"

I had to think about that one. "Well," I told him, "I'm not saying I'm sorry we did it, but I'm not sure it's really something I want to do again, you know?"

"Once is probably enough," he nodded.

"Yeah."

"The thing is, are you afraid to die?"

"Well, sort of," I said. On the TV, Todd Byrne realized that pieces of fire were falling on his head, and started smacking at his hair. It sort of looked like something you might see on *The Three Stooges*. "I'm afraid to die painfully, I guess."

"Fair enough. But how do you feel about losing all your shit?"

He had a point. I'd gotten all the stuff I really liked out

of the house before we left, but that didn't mean that I hated the stuff I left behind. In the back of my mind, I guess I hadn't realized that gone was *gone*. I hadn't just helped blow up our shithole house, I'd helped blow up my life. If things went our way, and it looked like they were going to, for all intents and purposes I had just killed myself. Officially, we'd be dead. That meant no more calls home for money, no more Thanksgiving dinners, no more birthday presents. It felt bad, but it felt pretty good, too.

We were dead. That meant we could do anything.

Plus, if you think about it, it's not like we were totally on our own. Or at least I wasn't. I had Lucas, and that guy will always look out for you, and not with a bunch of bitching and lectures like your parents do, either.

On the other hand, all Lucas had on his side was a guy who wasn't good for anything practical under the best of conditions and a chick who was currently passed out cold and bleeding from the crotch, so it didn't look too good for him. But if it didn't bother him, I sure wasn't going to waste any time worrying about it. He was probably used to it.

Let's face it--if you've had the kind of life where things look good for you very often and there's always somebody you can turn to when you need help, you don't turn out to be a guy like Lucas, do you?

"Hey," I said. "Where are we gonna go, when we can get moving again?"

"Patience, young Skywalker," he said, and gave me another one of those one-sided grins. "We're not done here yet."

"What do you mean?" I said. "We blew up the house, we've got all the shit we need. What else is there?"

"We've still got two more assholes to cross off my shitlist," he said.

That gave me a little jolt. The bad kind. And with Lucas, when you get the bad kind, it usually means the really good kind is just around the corner.

66

Dave

I had no idea that Lucas could cook. But he can, and he's good at it. Even better than my mom. And considering how much I like to eat, that's really saying something.

I was just going to eat a can of black olives I'd found in the pantry, but he started looking around and dragging out a whole bunch of stuff, and pretty soon he was whipping up an entire meal out of it. Seeing as how I'd known him for years and had never seen him do anything more strenuous than fry a hamburger, at first I thought he was just dicking around. Then he took a whole chicken out of the freezer and put it into a sink full of warm water to thaw it out, and I realized he was serious.

"Where the hell did you learn to cook?" I asked him.

"In a kitchen," he said.

Ask a stupid question… yadda yadda yadda.

"So do we have an actual plan for the last two names on your shitlist, or are we just gonna play it by ear?" I said. When you're embarrassed by your own stupidity, I find that the best thing to do is change the subject in a hurry and act like the whole thing never happened.

"There's a plan," he said. "I'm still working on it."

"What's with the chick?" I asked him. "Did you go check on her yet?"

He took a bag of potatoes--an actual *bag* of potatoes-- out of the bottom of the pantry and started peeling them. "She's not so good. Hurts more inside than outside, I think."

"That's weird," I said. "I didn't think she really wanted that kid anyway."

Lucas shrugged. "You never know. Things change." He cut the first peeled potato into quarters and dropped it in a pan of water beside the sink. "You should go hang out with her for a grip. Probably do her some good."

For a grip. I wasn't sure what that meant, but I assumed it meant "for a minute," or that for some reason completely foreign to me she needed something to grab onto and squeeze until it shrieked.

Either way, it didn't sound all that appealing.

"Look," I said. "It's not that I don't like her or anything? But the idea of talking to a chick when I know she's got crotch problems really freaks me out. It makes my brain feel all greasy and queasy, you know? I mean, I went with you when we bought that year's supply of cuntrags. Isn't that enough?"

From the look he gave me, I could tell that it wasn't.

"Come on," I said. "Don't you have like, wood I could chop, or a hole I could dig, or something manly like that instead?"

He dropped more potato chunks in the pot. "Suck it up," he told me. "She's our buddy. If Pete had gotten jumped and ass-fucked on his way home one night, and he was laying in bed with a bloody butt, you'd hang out with him wouldn't you?"

"That's not the same," I said. "I'd be making fun of him the whole time. I can't make fun of her. Not for this, anyway. That's too tasteless even for me."

Lucas lit a cigarette, took a drag, and balanced it on the edge of the sink. "Think of it as recon," he grinned.

I thought that was a really odd thing for him to say, but I have to admit it got my attention. "And what would I be trying to find out, exactly?" I asked.

"We're in a spot here," he told me. "She's got problems, one way or another. If it's medical, we'll wait it out and do what we can for her until she heals up."

"What if it's not medical?"

He dropped more chunks in the pot with a little splash and picked up his cigarette. "Then we deal with it another way and get the fuck out of Dodge," he said.

Another way. I wasn't sure what that meant, but I had a couple of ideas, and none of them looked too good for that chick. I thought about asking Lucas what he had in mind, exactly, but I just left it alone. It was his deal. If I needed to know, he'd tell me when the time came.

"I'll do it, Sarge," I told him. "Anything I should try to find out specifically?"

"Nah," he said. "Don't press anything. Just hang out

with her until I get the food on the table, and we'll hash it out later."

It had been so long since I ate real food that I couldn't remember how long it took to cook it, but I hoped it was quick. I didn't want to spend any more time with the Gyno Queen than I had to. And I was fucking starving.

67

Rachel

When Lucas called us I basically went down to the kitchen out of courtesy, although I was curious to see what he'd been up to. Eating was the last thing on my mind. Then my feet hit the linoleum, the smells went straight up my nose and into my brain, and I was ravenous. My mouth flooded with saliva and my stomach let out a growl that made all three of us laugh.

Lucas had laid out a spread that made me want to weep. Fried chicken, mashed potatoes and gravy, creamed peas, corn and homemade bread. All of it so fresh and hot that steam was still floating up toward the light that hung over the kitchen table. Dave and I stood there staring at each other, our mouths open like a couple of idiots.

"It's not gonna eat itself," Lucas said with one of his one-sided grins. "We better get on it."

So we got on it. And it was fantastic. Some of the best food I'd ever eaten in my life. I even ate the corn, and I hate corn. I copied the way Lucas ate it, which was to flatten out a little bowl in his mashed potatoes with the bottom of his spoon, put the corn in it, and then cover the whole thing with gravy. Not much to look at, but Jesus it tasted good. For twenty minutes nobody said anything; the only sounds in the room were silverware on plates and animal grunts of pleasure. I ate two helpings of everything and pushed back when I felt like I was going to throw it all up again if I took even one more bite. Dave, bottomless pit that he is, kept going.

Lucas lit two cigarettes and handed me one of them. "That gravy turned out better than I thought, considering I had to use powdered milk."

"That," I said, savoring the taste of the cigarette, "was incredible."

Dave licked at his fingers, his mouth still full. "Why the fuck would rich people have powdered milk?" he said.

No one had an answer for that, so we all just left it alone.

"You're an asshole," Dave said. "Seriously. If you know how to cook like this, why the hell have I been eating Ramen noodles for the last year? I'm making a new rule. You have to cook for me at least three times a week."

"No," Lucas said, with a bemused little smile on his face.

"It's not a yes-or-no question, it's a *rule*," Dave said. "That means you have to do it, because I say so."

"No," Lucas said again.

"What if we vote on it?" I said. "Because I'm totally with Dave on this one. That's two for and one against."

Dave gave me a gravy-covered thumbs-up. I'm sure he

would have said something, but he was stuffing more bread in his mouth.

"Still no good," Lucas told us.

"Why not?"

"Because the one against is the one you need to make the whole thing work," he grinned. "He's also the one who's not washing the dishes."

"Leave 'em," Dave grunted.

"We will," Lucas said. "Back in the cabinets. Clean."

I smiled at him. "Does anyone else find it strange that the one of us who eats the least is the one who knows how to cook?"

"It's food," Lucas shrugged. "You slop a bunch of stuff together in a pan and put some heat under it."

Dave's jaw dropped, which wasn't a sight anyone wanted to see. He held up one finger to save his place in the conversation and finished chewing. With his mouth closed, thank God.

"No no no," he said. "My *mom* slops a bunch of stuff together in a pan and puts heat under it. *This* is cooking. Seriously. Let's not diminish it with false modesty, okay? This was a fucking miracle on a plate."

"It was fantastic," I agreed. "But a miracle? I don't know if I'd go that far."

"Did you look around this kitchen before he started cooking?" Dave said. "Because I did. And I didn't see shit here that was worth eating. Then he comes in here like *The A-Team,* and an hour later we've got *this.* I don't think the word 'miracle' is much of a stretch."

I wanted to ask Lucas where he'd learned to cook like that--no matter what he said, it was a lot more than putting slop in a pan and heating it--but when I turned to look at him his bemused smile was gone. He was looking back at me as though he was fairly sure what was on my mind, and he didn't want any part of it. Not that he was giving me a glare or anything. It's just that his whole face had gone neutral and his eyes were doing what they usually do-- telling you *no* by virtue of not telling you anything else.

Dave, seeing that nobody else was calling dibs, had pulled the gravy bowl in front of him and was dipping bread into it. "Yeah, so I found this porn?" he said, using a hunk of crust to break up the skin that was forming on the top of the bowl. "And I was watching it, because I'm guy? And I had this huge, mind-blowing revelation."

I knew I shouldn't do it, but I had to. "Which was...?"

He gave me the most sincere look I've ever seen him give. Not fake-sincere, either. "Watching somebody eat pussy is *really* boring."

I don't know what was funnier--that he would say something like that, apropos of nothing, or that in some way this qualified as a mind-blowing revelation in his mind. Either way, I laughed until tears were rolling down my face and I had a stitch in my side.

My laughter didn't faze him a bit. "Yeah," he said. "It's like, you think something would be really hot about it, cause it's like, you know, *eating pussy*. But mostly it always just looks like somebody eating soft-serve ice cream in a nursing home."

Lucas, his chair tipped back on two legs like he was waiting to get out of study hall on a Friday afternoon, grinned. "And if it looks like it's got sprinkles on it, you should probably leave it alone," he said.

Sometimes, when there's not much else going on in my head, I think about the friends I've had. Almost all of them-- and all of the really good ones--have been guys. They're genuine. They laugh at what they think is funny, no matter what anybody else thinks. There's no politics involved. They're loyal to each other, and if you don't play games and are able to keep your end up, they're loyal to you, too. I mean, I'm almost positive that it was a guy who came up with the theory of taking one for the team. A girl would never think like that. At least none of the ones I've known.

Dave looked at the gravy bowl one last time, grimaced, and pushed it away. He lit a Marlboro Light from a new pack beside his plate and looked at Lucas. "How's that plan coming?"

"I've had better," Lucas said.

I groaned. "Is this ever going to end? Seriously. Every time I think we're done and we can just go, there's something else."

They looked at me. "I hate to break it to you, dolly, but this time you're part of the something else," Dave said.

"What?"

"I'm not gonna throw you in the car and ride all over hell like this," Lucas said. "You're not up to snuff. It's not worth it."

"I'll be fine," I told them. "You're right, I feel like shit.

But my discomfort aside, we gotta go. I'm a big girl. I'll tough it out."

"I know you will," Lucas said. "I know you could. But that don't mean I'm in a hurry to make you do it."

For a man well-versed in all things literary, the way Lucas talks leaves something to be desired, grammatically. You don't really notice it when you're in the moment, but when you're replaying it in your mind, it sort of tickles you.

"Well, give me some pain-killers, throw that bale of maxi-pads you bought me in the trunk, and let's do it anyway," I said. "As long as I don't have to chase anybody around for a week or two, I'm good."

"Jesus Christ," Dave muttered. "A *bale*. And it was, too."

Lucas stubbed out his cigarette on the edge of his plate and stood up. "Go to bed," he said. "We get these dishes done, we're going too."

"I'm not tired," Dave said.

"Get tired," Lucas told him. "We've got a bunch of shit to do tomorrow, we start early, and I don't want anybody dragging ass."

68

<u>Dave</u>

My all-time vote for more balls than brains?

Frenchie the Fridge didn't lock his door.

Now I didn't know him that well--and let's be honest, who the fuck would want to? But he sort of seemed like the kind of guy who would leave his door open in the hopes that somebody would try to break in just so he could shoot them. He had like three guns in his bedroom, all of them within easy reach. Not that it mattered.

Lucas stood right over him, staring down at him. Grinning. I was by the bedroom door, in case something went bad and I had to make a break for it. And before you start thinking I'm chickenshit, I should point out that it's what Lucas told me to do.

Frenchie the Fridge was sound asleep in his underoos, sprawled out on his back, mouth open, sawing logs. Apparently running around like a chicken with its head cut off, looking for assholes like us and watching people try to put out the fire we'd started, that takes a lot out of you. The curtains were drawn, and room had this whole dim, clammy, body-odor kind of vibe that was pretty sleazy.

I don't know how long Lucas stood over him like that. It seemed like ten minutes, but it wasn't. Then he hawked one up, way back in his throat, and spit a loogie right in Frenchie's face. That fucking pig's eyes snapped open at the sound of it, just in time to catch the wad right in his eyeball.

"Morning," Lucas said, all soft and lilting like somebody's mom. Then he drilled Frenchie right in the face and knocked him out cold.

He held out his gloved hand and I tossed him the rope we'd found in the garage at our new clubhouse. We trussed the Fridge up tight--elbows, wrists, knees and ankles, with a loop around his neck that tied off to the one around his feet. Lucas used a bunch of knots I'd never even seen before, but they looked pretty brutal. The he took a pair of dirty whitey-tighties off the floor, jammed them in Frenchie's mouth, and covered them with duct tape.

"We're on the clock," Lucas told me. He was jerking a case off of one of the pillows and pulling it over Frenchie's head. "Look for files, papers, anything that might have anything to do with us. I doubt there's anything here, but check it all. Keep it quiet, and try not to make too much of a mess."

69

Rachel

When I woke up the house was empty. There was a note on the kitchen table, under the Camaro keys and half a pack of cigarettes, written in Lucas' writing, which is a strange hybrid of block-printing and cursive that's easy to read and oddly pretty to look at.

We'll be back. Worse comes to worse, you got kidnapped. I'll make you breakfast--

And then it was signed, if you could call it that, with a quick little picture of a skull. No bottom jaw, no crossbones.

I've had more elaborate love-notes, if you could call it that. But none of them made me giddy and put tears in my eyes at the same time like that one did. I held it up to my nose to see if it smelled like him somehow, but it just smelled like blank white paper.

They'd left a bag beside the bathroom door; when I looked inside I found it was filled with my clothes.

Apparently they'd raided my apartment while I was passed out in the car, the softies. I took a long hot shower, got myself together, and plopped down in front of the TV with a can of Mountain Dew and the smokes and waited.

I was halfway through an episode of *Columbo*--one that starred Johnny Cash, which was way cool--when I heard a vehicle coming up the drive. After peeking out the window to make sure that it was Lucas, driving the truck the Chicago people had left parked in the garage, and that there was nobody following him, I went out on the porch to meet them.

As soon as the truck came to a complete stop, Dave rolled over the far side of the bed with a gun in his hand. "Don't look, I gotta whiz," he said, already unzipping himself with his free hand. "God*damn* it's cold back there."

"You should have a coat on," Lucas told me, and looked into the bed of the truck. "They give you any shit?"

"Nah," Dave said, and groaned as he finished. "If we ever do this again, I'm driving. *You* sit back there and freeze your ass off. I'll be lucky if I don't crap my kidneys out next time I go."

"You can't drive," I said.

He looked at me. "I'll figure it out. And before you even get started, I don't wanna hear it, Miss I-Get-To-Stay-In-A-Nice-Warm-Bed-And-Sleep."

Lucas dropped the tailgate and motioned me forward. There were four bodies and a small beige two-drawer file cabinet wedged into the bed. Dave held the gun out to me. "It's loaded," he said.

"What am I supposed to do with it?" I said.

"Any of them moves, shoot 'em in the fucking head," Lucas told me.

"The head being the end with the pillowcase on it," Dave smirked.

Lucas wrapped his arms around the file cabinet and picked it up with the drawers facing his chest. "Somebody get the door."

He and Dave took the cabinet inside and came back. "Alright, listen up," he said, and slapped a hand against the truck. "I'm gonna pull you out one at a time and stand you up. Stay where I put you. Keep your mouths shut. Anybody moves, anybody talks, they get shot in the stomach."

The first two bodies he pulled out were female. He was gentle. He nodded toward them, and I turned the gun in their direction. They were shivering, but they didn't move.

He grabbed the other two by the ropes around their ankles and yanked them back in one lunge. They hit the ground on their backs and let out muffled groans. "Shotgun," he said.

Dave took a pump-action out of the front seat of the truck and held it on them.

Lucas leaned forward, put a shoulder into each of the women's waists, and picked them up like they were oversized teddy bears, with their torsos draped over his back. "Come on," he said, and I followed him into the house.

He deposited them on the couch where I'd been camped

out and pulled the pillowcases off of their heads. They blinked at us like two owls, their eyes watery but not what I would call crying. They were still shivering; I could hear their teeth chattering behind the duct tape over their mouths. One of them looked 16. The other one was probably close to 40, but looked younger.

Lucas knelt down in front of them. "Listen to me now," he said, his voice softer than it had been by the truck. "You behave yourselves, we'll treat you good. You wanna fuck around and pitch a fit, go ahead. But that'll put you on my bad side. And that's not somewhere you want to be. We understand each other?"

They nodded.

"I'm gonna pull the tape off your mouths. It'll hurt. There's no way around that. You stay on my good side, and I can guarantee you it's the last pain you're gonna feel today. Yeah?"

They nodded again.

"Count of three," he said. He counted off and ripped. They cringed, but neither of them made a peep. A tear rolled down the older one's cheek, and he swiped it away with a delicate finger. "Go ahead a lean back, get as comfortable as you can. I've got a couple of things to take care of, but I'll be back to untie you in a few minutes."

He stood up, wiping his wet finger on his jeans. "No talking, now."

"Be back," he told me. One corner of his mouth was a little higher than the other, and I wanted to kiss him so bad I could taste it.

70

<u>Dave</u>

I'd naturally assumed that getting those two cops in the house would involve untying them, or at least parts of them. Lucas had another idea. He grabbed the ropes around their ankles and dragged them both around the side of the house to the basement door. At the same time. He had to strain a little, but not much. There was some pissed-off, through-clenched-teeth grunting, but he didn't stop to rest or anything.

Their heads made a sound that was kind of cool, bouncing off every wooden step on the way down, but it was nothing to write home about. Actually, I was sort of hoping for something that sounded a little more dramatic. Apparently they just make that shit up for TV.

We'd laid out some plastic sheeting under two dining room chairs, and tied them to those. When he was sure they weren't going anywhere, he locked the basement door and we went back up to the living room.

Lucas pulled out his big redneck buck knife and started cutting the ropes of the chicks. "Sir?" the older one said. Her voice was all shaky. "I'm sorry, but I really need to use the restroom."

"Nothing to be sorry about," he told her. "The thing is, my friend Rachel's gonna have to go with you."

"She's going to *watch* me?" the lady said.

Lucas grinned. "Don't worry, she's a good kid. We don't know each other that well yet, you and me. If she goes with you, I don't have to wait on you and wonder if you're doing something that's gonna put you on my bad side. Okay?"

"Okay," she said. She didn't look happy about it, but she was smart enough to realize she didn't have any choice.

So they went. The jeans that chick was wearing didn't do much for her, but you kind of got the idea that if you got her naked she'd probably look really good, for somebody's mom. It was the kind of thought that my penis and I could devote some quality time to later. But at the moment, both of us were too tired to deal with it.

"Dude, are you checking out my mom's ass?" the younger chick said.

"More or less," I nodded, and started checking her out instead. Total goth-jailbait. Dyed-black hair with cherry red streaks in it, too much mascara. A Tool concert shirt and a lot of bracelets and rings.

"I gotta piss too," she said. "Only when I go, I want you to go with me." She grinned. "I like it when guys check out my ass."

Lucas gave me a look. It wasn't encouraging.

"I think I liked her better when she couldn't talk," I said. "At least then I could pretend she had a brain and a personality."

"*Whatever*," the chick said, and rolled her eyes.

Apparently brains and personality still aren't cool with the high school crowd.

"Don't talk," Lucas told her. "It'll be less painful."

He re-tied her ankles with about two feet of rope between them so she could hobble around, but she couldn't kick anybody. I personally thought it was a wise move. She looked like a kicker.

"What the fuck?" she said. "My mom don't have to walk around like this."

He grabbed two fistfuls of her hair and pulled her face to his. "If you talk again without raising your hand and getting permission, I'm gonna strip you, tie you spread-eagle on a bed, and put out lit cigarettes on your asshole," he told her.

He shoved her back down on the couch and looked at her. She rubbed the sides of her head and scowled at him with teary eyes, but she kept her mouth shut. "I'm gonna take care of the truck," he told me. "If she moves or opens her mouth, break her nose."

Rachel and the little chick's mom came back. "This one has to go too," I said.

"So take her," Rachel said.

"Yeah, that was her idea too," I said. "But I think you better do it."

She sighed. "Come on, Vampira."

"Apparently she likes having her ass checked out while she's going," I said. "Be careful. Don't get any on you."

The chick's mom groaned and started rubbing the bridge of her nose, the classic I'm-so-ashamed-of-my-offspring gesture. You could sort of see where she was coming from. It's not exactly good hostage etiquette to offer your kidnappers a golden shower show right off the bat. At least I don't think it is. Then again, I'd never kidnapped anybody before, so the whole thing was just full of surprises.

71

<u>Rachel</u>

That girl was a real piece of work.

"You into girls at all, or are you all about the cock?" she said as she was taking her pants down.

"Pardon me?"

"Pussy," she said, and flicked at her clit. "You ever get with another chick?"

"No," I said.

"I like both," she smiled. "I mean, I like a big fat cock in me, but every once in awhile, you just get a craving, you know?"

"How old are you?" I said.

"Fifteen." I could hear the water streaming out of her. "Does it matter?"

I didn't have an answer for that. At least not one that wouldn't make me feel old and really, really uncool. I tried to remember if I'd had cravings to go down on another girl or for having "a big fat cock in me" when I was 15, but I couldn't really come up with anything.

"Whatever," she said. "All I know is, if you're gonna kill me, I wanna get fucked *hard* before I go. *Really* hard. That's only fair, right?"

"You're barking up the wrong tree," I told her. "I don't do girls." Dave only did dead ones, as far as I knew, which wouldn't do her any good. What Lucas did or didn't do was still anybody's guess.

She patted herself dry and stood up. "Tell me something, just between us girls. Your friend, the big one? I bet he's got a huge cock. Most big guys are hung like a light switch, but he seems like the type to be packing some serious meat."

"What makes you say that?" I frowned. I'd thought about sleeping with Lucas several times, but I'd never given much thought to the size of him below the belt. It just hadn't occurred to me.

"I dunno," she shrugged as she flushed. The toilet, I mean. I think the only way you could have gotten that little whore's face to turn red is to put your hands around her throat and choke the shit out of her. Which, all things considered, was an idea I was getting more excited about by the minute. "He's kind of got that confidence, you know? Guys with little ones are always trying to impress you somehow. You can tell that they doubt themselves. He doesn't carry himself like that."

Which is true, to a point. Lucas is the prime example of absolute confidence--I've never seen a shadow of a doubt in him, ever. Whether or not that has anything to do with the size of his package, I don't know. It was something to think about, anyway.

"Free advice?" I told her as she washed her hands. "Don't talk to him about sex. I can guarantee it won't go well for you."

She rolled her eyes at me in the mirror. "Are you fucking kidding me? I'm fifteen, horny, I've got big tits and

I love taking it up the ass. I'm like, an American wet dream, or something."

To quote Dave:

Jesus Fucking Christ.

72

Dave

Lucas came back in with a bag of groceries I had totally forgotten about stopping for on our way to get the cops, which just goes to show you how distracting bloodlust can be. We brought the chicks into the kitchen and sat them down at the table so we could keep an eye on them, and he started making pancakes.

"Total fucking *whore*," Rachel said to me under her breath, nodding toward the little chick. "I can't *wait* to tell you what we talked about in the bathroom."

"Sir?" the mom said. Looking at Lucas, of course. Always the dominant gorilla in the cage, that guy. "I hate to bother you, but I don't suppose you have any Valium?"

Lucas, who was stirring batter with a wire whisk, looked up at her. "Valium," he said. And the word just sort of hung there.

Vampira started laughing. "My mommy's a fucking pill-head," she said. "Isn't that precious?"

Lucas sat the bowl down on the counter and picked up a roll of duct tape. "Hold her head," he said.

I wanted to do it, but Mrs. Lucas beat me to the punch. She did it with enthusiasm, too--definitely some sort of gyno-political going on there. Luke slapped tape over the little chick's mouth and wrapped her wrists. "You're not very bright," he told her. "Last chance. Remember what I told you. I wasn't kidding."

That chick's mom looked like she had the beginnings of a killer migraine setting in. "I'm so sorry," she said. "Gretchen has... problems."

Lucas lit a cigarette. I could tell by the way he nodded at her that Gretchen might not have problems much longer if she didn't straighten the fuck up and do what she was told. "I might have some Valium. If not, I could get you something else. Vicodin, maybe."

She looked like she wanted to hug him. "I'm sure that would be fine. Thank you."

He got his bag of Magic Beans out of the fridge and sifted through it until he found what he was looking for. He set five pills on the table with a glass of water. "We need to make a deal."

She looked at him, at the freezer bag, at the pills in front of her, and at him again. It was sort of pathetic. "Okay."

"I need you to hold it together. If you float so far off into la-la land that it causes me problems--"

"I won't," she said. "I promise I won't."

He nodded at her and she took two of the pills, swallowed them, glanced at Lucas, and took another. "That should do it," she said, and forced a smile. "Should I just put these others in my pocket, or--?"

"Let's leave them on the table," he said, and went back to his stirring. "Nobody'll bother them."

"You're not what I expected," she said, and patted at her hair. "Somehow I always pictured you as... well, cruel."

"I am."

She cringed a little. "Oh."

He chased lumps around the mixing bowl with the whisk and tapped it off on the rim. We were all so quiet that the sound seemed louder than it actually was. "What's your name?"

"Alison."

Lucas spooned some butter onto the fancy griddle that was built into the island in the center of the kitchen and watched it sizzle. "I make them thick, Alison. How many do you want?"

73

Dave

After breakfast, Lucas put Mrs. Lucas and the cop's wife on dish detail. He left Vampira tied and gagged--no pancakes for her. Her loss. I don't know how one would go about rating pancakes, exactly, but they were good.

We slipped down the basement stairs and stood there, watching the cops try to get free. They weren't having much success, but they it wasn't for lack of effort. Lucas cleared his throat and they froze. He took the pillowcases off of their heads and ripped the tape off their faces. Frenchie the Fridge spat his dirty underwear out of his mouth and looked pretty much like anybody would look if they'd been forced to taste their own skid-marks for two hours, but he didn't say anything.

"I want answers," Lucas told them.

Reisman laughed. I don't know if it was a nervous reaction, or if he was just trying to pretend he was a tough guy to hide how scared he was. Either way it wasn't very convincing.

"Why should I tell you anything?" he said.

Lucas lit a cigarette. "You don't talk, or I catch you lying to me, I'll torture you."

Both of the pigs snorted at him. Literally. I still don't understand what that was about. How far can you take the jaded tough-guy act? We'd gone into their houses, beat the shit out of them, kidnapped them, and had them tied to chairs. One of them was in his underwear. And they were still trying to bluff us, the fucking idiots.

Personally, I was offended. But you can't offend Lucas on purpose. He sees right through it, and ignores it like he does every other distraction.

"If that doesn't do it for you, remember that I've got your wife and daughter here. Right now they're happy. I fed them, I gave your wife some pills. Nice lady. Talks too much when she's high, but I like her."

Reisman flinched.

"You play ball with me, I dope them up, they fall asleep, and they just don't wake up. Painless." Luke was starting to get that cobra look in his eye, and it sobered them up quick. He had their full attention, and there wasn't anything that even resembled a smirk on either of their faces. "You want to fuck around and play games, they're gonna suffer.

And I'll make sure that they know you're the reason for it. You've seen our work. We'll do your daughter, right in front of your wife. Then we'll do your wife, right in front of you. She'll know it was your fault. I'll make sure of that."

"*Fuck you!*" Reisman spat. It's the most pissed-off I've ever seen a guy. After Lucas, of course. "You pathetic, degenerate fucking *scumbag.*"

"Degenerate maybe," I said. "But since you're tied to a chair and about to get your ass kicked, I'd say that makes you way more pathetic than we are."

"First question," Lucas said. "Anybody think we're still alive?"

You could see the wheels spinning in Reisman's head, but he came up with nothing. "Nobody knows," he said. "After that shit you pulled last night, nobody knows anything."

"They'll be looking for the car."

"Eventually," Reisman said. "That was the first thing I was going to start on this morning."

Lucas nodded. "Evidence. What have you got on us?"

"We don't know yet."

Lucas punched him in the nose. Not hard enough to break it, just enough to get the blood flowing and make his eyes water. "You wanna try again?"

"There's too much of it," Reisman said. "We're backlogged. We've got people working round-the-clock on it, but so far there's nothing that points to either of you specifically."

Another point for my man Lucas. According to him,

sorority houses and college rent houses in general were the best places in the world to do what we did. None of them were cleaned that well or that often, and people were in and out of there all the time. No matter how careful you are, you're going to leave a trace of yourself behind. Stray hairs, fingerprints, whatever. But in the places we went, whatever we left was mixed in with the traces of everybody else who had been there. Hit a house with four or five people living in it, add up all their friends who stop by, not to mention whoever might show up to any little social gathering they might be having, and we're just another grain of salt in the shaker. Each grain has to be catalogued and tracked back to its source, which in our case made the whole thing impossible. And when people starting running back home to mommy and daddy, it just made it that much harder.

"So all that stuff about the security cameras at Wal-Mart was just bullshit," I said.

Reisman gave me a dirty look.

I noticed my shoe was untied. I bent over, tied it, and punched Frenchie the Fridge in the balls on the way back up. "Should have called no-touchbacks," I told him. Then I nutted him again. Three seconds later he puked all down the front of himself, which was sort of freaky. I didn't know a shot in the balls could make you do that.

Lucas lit another cigarette. "Which part of this situation don't you understand?" he said. "I thought I made it clear, but I can go over it again."

Nobody said anything. The Fridge was still try to spit the taste out of his mouth, and his hairy gut was flexing involuntarily. Not a pretty sight, let me tell you.

Lucas pulled out that big buck-knife of his and flicked it open. "We ask, you answer. Quickly. Don't stop and think about it. They're all questions you know the answers to. You pause, it tells me you're trying to find the right pile of bullshit to shovel in our direction. And the next time the words 'I don't know' come out of your mouth, I'm gonna start slicing patches of skin off."

I actually saw the veins pop in Reisman's temples. "Yeah," he said. "I got it. You're in charge, chief."

Chief. Lucas and I raised our eyebrows at each other. He didn't get it, not yet. But he was gonna.

Lucas opened the top drawer of the filing cabinet we'd taken from Reisman's house and took out a handful of folders. He dropped them on top of the washing machine, opened the first folder, and began to read. His eyes moved back and forth in fast, easy patterns. If it had been anybody else, I would have sworn they were just pretending to read and called bullshit on them.

"I'm gonna get a Mountain Dew," I said. "You want one?"

He gave me a one-sided grin, and I knew we were still in business. "Sure," he said. "Let her know we'll be awhile, and we don't want to be disturbed."

74

Rachel

Occasionally Dave would come up from the basement to

grab a couple more sodas or something to eat, but I was never quite sure what was going on down there. I couldn't ask him, because I was on guard detail, which meant that I had to keep a close eye on the other two, and he didn't want to say anything in front of them.

Alison took the last two pills Lucas had left on the kitchen table for her and just sort of turned into a softly-giggling lump on the couch. I put soap operas on the TV and she was like a baby with a fresh bottle. It was sort of sad, really.

Gretchen still had her hands and mouth taped. She spent the better part of an hour glaring at me, until I got sick of it and dumped her out of the recliner she'd been sitting in and made her lie on her stomach. I had a feeling she was going to be trouble before it was all over, and I didn't know if I was up to it.

After Dave had wandered through the living room for the third time, shoving Doritos into his mouth, Alison yawned. "I feel like there was something I was supposed to *do,*" she said, and frowned. "What time is Mike coming to pick us up?"

"Mike?" I said.

"My husband."

Have you ever looked at somebody who was drunk or drugged-up and wanted to punch them in the face, just to see if it was still possible for anything to get through the haze they'd put themselves in? That's what I wanted to do to her then. I mean, how comfortably numb do you need to be?

"He didn't say," I told her.

"Oh." She looked back at the TV and her face instantly reverted to its normal state of pleasant confusion.

Gretchen was craning her neck to look back at us. She was still glaring, but there was something else in it. And for once she wasn't spreading the hate around. Her mom was getting all of it.

"If I sit you up and take the tape off of your mouth, are you gonna behave?" I said.

She gave me an annoyed, distracted look, and nodded. I pulled her over and helped her to her feet. The skin around her mouth was red when I pulled the duct tape off. "I have to pee again," she said. Quietly. "And I wanna talk to your friend. It's important."

"I already told you--"

"Not about *that*," she said. "Something else. Just ask him if he'll talk to me."

There were a dozen reasons I could think of *not* to do it. But it was like something had changed about her since we'd brought her in, and I sort of wanted to see what would happen. The whole Lolita-thing was gone. She looked like she actually had something to say.

"Stay put," I said, and opened the door that led to the basement. "Dave," I called down. "Could you come here for a minute?"

"Not *him*," she hissed. "The other one."

I held a finger up and she shut her mouth. Dave came upstairs and shut the door behind him with a soft click. He looked around the room, trying to see what the trouble was.

"What's up?" he said.

"She wants to talk to Lucas," I said. I kept my voice down.

Dave looked at Gretchen, and something flickered behind his glasses that made me uncomfortable. "About what?"

"I don't know, but she seems pretty serious about it."

He shrugged. "I'll tell him, but don't get your hopes up. He's in the middle of something."

A few minutes later Lucas came up, wiping something off of his hands with a stained towel. He tucked the towel into his back pocket and came into the living room. He might have been annoyed. It's hard to tell.

"One of our guests would like to have a word with you," I said.

"What about?"

"I don't know," I said, "but I've got a feeling you're gonna wanna hear her out. She looks pretty determined."

He gave the girl a look I hope he never gives me. She squirmed.

"What about the other one?" he said.

"She's all fucked-up," I told him. "Way over the rainbow. Are you sure those were valium?"

He leaned around me to check out Alison, who was sprawled out on the leather couch in a very un-ladylike position and doing something strange with her lips. "The first three were."

"What about the other two?"

He grinned. "Something else."

I smiled back at him. I wouldn't have thought of it, but it made sense--if she was going to try to take them all, it meant she was a dope-head, and that was potential trouble. Whatever the other two had been, they messed her up good. She was still functional. Beyond that, she seemed to be in a docile state of retardation. No trouble at all.

Dave had come up the stairs and was looking at us through a gap he'd opened in the door. "Hang loose," Lucas told him. "We gotta do something."

We followed Gretchen into the bathroom and shut the door behind us. As soon as Lucas cut the tape off her hands she dropped her pants and sat down, the water flowing out of her.

"*Jesus*," she said. "I thought I was gonna wet myself."

Lucas opened the mirrored medicine cabinet over the sink and started checking its contents. "You wanted something?"

"I thought I could talk to you alone," she said.

Lucas plucked a package of ancient, rusting razor blades out of the cabinet and laid them on the counter. "She's with me," he said. "If you can't say it in front of her, I don't need to hear it."

She's with me. It was enough to make my palms sweat. In a perfect world, I would have jumped up, put my arms around his neck, and kissed him for hours. But it's not a perfect world, that wasn't the time or place, and I wasn't sure if there *was* a time or place for that with him. The more I wanted it, the less likely it seemed.

She gave me look that had a shot of jealousy in it, which

is always good for a girl's self-esteem. "I know what the deal is," she said. "I'm not *stupid.*"

That particular fact was still up for debate, but neither of us bothered.

"I know you're gonna kill my dad, and that fucking asshole Frenchie, too. Neither one of them is any big loss." She was silent until Lucas pulled the medicine cabinet door toward himself and looked at her. "I want to watch."

One side of Lucas' mouth eased back. "Oh yeah?"

"I'm not kidding. I wanna watch you do it, and I hope you do it fucking *slow.*"

Lucas pulled a tube of Icy-Hot out of the cabinet and laid it next to the razor blades. "Sure you don't want to do it yourself? I've got him trussed up like a hog down there. Nothing to it."

Gretchen shuddered, and we could hear another squirt hit the water in the bowl. "If I thought I could, I would," she told him, and her voice got soft. "But I don't think I've got the guts for it."

Lucas shut the cabinet, lit a cigarette, and sat on the edge of the sink. "I'm using you against him," he said. "He's only telling me what I want to know because he thinks it's gonna keep you from getting hurt. He gets the idea you want to watch him die, he might clam up. And then none of you are any good to me."

She pulled the front of her TOOL shirt over her knees and shivered. "I've seen stuff," she said. "Pictures and video and stuff. He doesn't keep his office locked, cause he thinks nobody gives a shit about his work. And we don't.

But I found some of it one time when I was looking for the key to the liquor cabinet, and I had to see it. I mean, what-- you're gonna have shit like that right in your own house, and not even try to take a peek? But I've seen the stuff you do. It's fucking *crazy*."

The way she said it, "crazy" was not an insult.

If I'm going to be honest--and let's face it, it's a little late in the game to get bashful now--the way she said it made me want to beat her to death with an axe-handle. Right there on the toilet with her pants around her ankles. Little Miss American Wet Dream, sitting there with her self-worth showing, batting her thick black lashes at what was mine, after I *told* her not to.

Lucas is not mine. He's not anybody's. He just *is*. But I had my cap set for him, as my grandma used to say, and that little bitch was trying to mark my territory.

Love ain't always pretty, boys and girls.

Sometimes it's enough to make you wanna kill.

"I'll think about it," Lucas shrugged. He flipped a little pill of ash into the sink and watched it roll toward the drain before getting hung up on a drop of water and turn to black paste. "No promises."

Her shivering was getting worse--the lid on the toilet tank was beginning to chatter. "You're one scary fucking dude," she said.

It was so quiet I could hear the end of Lucas' cigarette crackle as he took another drag and exhaled.

"No shit," she said. "I ain't scared of nothing, you can ask anybody that knows me. I'm a tough chick. I'll fight anybody, I don't give a fuck. Guys, girls, whatever. But I never seen anything like you, ever."

"Let's go," he said, and turned his head away to give her what privacy he could while she finished up.

75

Dave

When I was a kid, my parents had the oldies station on the radio every time we got in the car to go somewhere. Trying to relive their youth, or whatever. There was this one song they played on there all the time, "Bad, Bad Leroy Brown," I think was the name of it. Sort of cheesy, but you could get into it if you weren't in a real pisser, stuck-in-a-rolling-jail kind of mood. It had this one line I always remember-- "old Leroy looked like a jigsaw puzzle with a couple of pieces gone."

It's a pretty good line, gives you a definite mental image when you hear it. Not the kind of thing you think you'll ever see in real life, though. Then again, most people probably never will.

Most people don't hang around with Lucas.

When he told Reisman that if the words "I don't know," came out of his mouth again, he would start slicing patches of skin off, he meant it. And apparently, Reisman is a little slow on the up-take. You'd think he would've caught on after the first one, but maybe the pain was clouding his brain. You can't really hold that against the guy.

Well, maybe you shouldn't, anyway.

Luke took the first one off of his chest, hair and all, about four inches square. We stuck Frenchie's underwear in his mouth so the chicks wouldn't hear him scream, I put his head in a bear-hold, and Luke started cutting. It was a little rough, but for a first attempt it looked pretty good. The ones after that got better by leaps and bounds. We took one off his right bicep, one off his left thigh, another off each of his sides. By the time we got to the love handles, they were perfectly square. If you took a couple steps back he looked like a patchwork quilt that somebody had scrounged out of a dumpster behind a butcher shop. It probably didn't help that we'd cut his clothes off because it was easier than untying him.

Frenchie got his, too, but not with the knife. Every time he opened his mouth when he wasn't supposed to, or said something stupid, Luke punched him in the face. His nose was broken, he was missing teeth, and one of his eyes was swollen shut. You'd think a guy would learn. I know I would have shut the fuck up after the first couple. Lucas had hit me a couple of times, just screwing around, and that shit hurts. Compared to what he was doing to Frenchie, all I got were love-taps.

Lucas came back from dealing with the chicks and dropped some stuff on top of the dryer. "Have a nice time playing with yourself, shitbag?" Frenchie asked him.

Lucas punched him in his broken nose, and blood splattered. He shook his hand to loosen it up, his fingers slapping together.

Frenchie coughed and snorted and drooled blood down

his chest and stomach. "What's the matter? Hurt your hand?"

One side of Lucas' mouth went up. "Stung a little," he said. "You wanna hear the bad news?"

The Fridge just stared at him.

"I've been hitting you with my left hand," Lucas said. "But I'm right-handed. I haven't started with the good one yet."

You could see the fight gurgle out of Frenchie like a waterbed mattress with the plug pulled. He didn't have much left.

Reisman's mouth was still jawing away at the dirty skivvies. Either he was trying to scream or he was starting to get into the taste. His face was a bad shade of red, and between the tears running down it and the sweat popping off of it, he looked like a grease fire waiting to happen.

Lucas picked up a gallon jug of water and nudged Frenchie's bare shin with the toe of his boot. "You thirsty?"

"Yeah."

"Tilt your head back. I'll pour it slow."

He gave him a mouthful of water, which Frenchie held for too long.

"Go on and spit it out," Lucas told him. "Just don't do anything stupid."

The Fridge turned his head to the side and basically let it fall out of his mouth. It splattered out pink on the plastic and ran toward the legs of his chair. "One more time," Lucas said, and they repeated it. Then Frenchie drank until Luke cut him off.

"Not too much," he said. "You might cramp up."

Frenchie nodded. "What about Mike?"

"In a minute." Lucas capped the jug and handed it to me. "You guys are buddies?"

"We're partners." Frenchie looked us over. "Like you two. Only we're on the other side."

Lucas nodded and squatted down on his haunches. "The other side of what?"

"The line. Between good and evil."

I had to laugh at that. I hadn't said anything for awhile, hadn't even cleared my throat, and it sounded like a weird, raspy hyena chuckle. Kind of cool, actually. If I could figure out how to make that sound all the time, I probably would.

The cops stared at me like I was about to go apeshit on them. I looked at Lucas, and he was grinning. With both sides of his mouth.

"That's what you're gonna go with on this one?" I said. "Good and evil?"

Frenchie didn't say anything.

"You're the good, and we're the evil. That's how you've got it figured out?"

"Yeah," Frenchie said. His one good eye was glaring at me for all it was worth, which was more than you'd think. "You probably take that as a compliment, scumbag. But you're *less* than evil. You're just a sick, sleazy little worm that nobody ever got around to stepping on. You're lower than dogshit."

"Thanks," I smiled. "Most of the time, the thing that's

lower than dogshit is pretty green grass. One of God's beautiful miracles. You're not very well-spoken, but I guess a compliment is a compliment."

"You're pathetic," Frenchie spat. "A disgusting little pervert. You can talk your crazy bullshit circles all you want, but you know what you are. You sick, twisted *fuck.*"

I sat down on the floor in front of him, Indian-style. The cement floor was cold on my ass, but not unbearable. "Go on buddy," I nodded. "Get it all out. You'll feel better."

"You're *garbage*," he said. "You're not fit to breathe the same air as human beings. I've been there when they clean up the fucking messes you leave behind. All those good kids, ripped apart and raped, just because your mommy and daddy wouldn't buy you a Nintendo for your birthday and the big kids used to give you wedgies and stuff you in your fucking gym locker."

Nice little speech, I thought. It probably would have been more effective if he'd directed it at both of us instead of just the one who was less likely to beat him to death with his bare hands, but all in all, a nice attempt.

"How do you know they were good?" I said. "Have you got some sort of inside information on them that I don't know about? Cause I might have been wrong, but they all seemed like worthless fucking cunts to me. I mean, it's a little late now, but I'm always willing to listen to a good argument."

Boy, was he *mad*. He was straining against the ropes so hard the chair was creaking. "What gives you the right?" he said. He wasn't yelling yet, but he was working up to it.

"What gives you the fucking right to do that to people?"

"Nobody gave it to me," I said. "I took it. Just like you did. The difference is, I'm not some chickenshit who needed to sign up for a badge and a gun and kiss the right ass and pretend to want to help other people. I don't have to wait around and hope that maybe a few times things will go my way and I might get to shoot somebody I don't like. I don't daydream about everybody calling me a hero and pinning a cheap medal on me and patting my head like a good little doggie who learned to crap in the garden instead of on the rug."

"You don't know what the fuck you're talking about."

"*You* don't know what the fuck I'm talking about," I told him. "It's not the same thing."

"You're fucking insane."

"Probably. But let me ask you this--how come you became a cop in the first place? I bet it was because you wanted to make a difference, right? Wanted to make the world a better place, and all that?"

He didn't say anything, but that glare got cranked up a notch. It looked like he was headed for Stroke City. I sort of wanted to see if I could get his eyeball to pop without touching it, but it seemed like the kind of thing you needed a definite plan for, and I was too lazy to come up with one.

Besides, eyeball-popping is a good hands-on experience, and there aren't really enough of those in life to waste.

"Hey, you can say it," I told him. "I'm not gonna laugh at you. Stuff like that sounds cheesy, but it's not cheesy if it's true. So level with me. That's what you're about, right?"

"Yeah," he said. "That's what I'm about. And I'm not ashamed of it."

"Well you know what? So are we. And we're not ashamed of it either. We take good-for-nothing assholes who make this world a shitty place, and we eliminate them."

"You're fucking insane," Frenchie said.

"And you're repeating yourself," I told him. "You really should have invested in a thesaurus while you had time."

"You don't deserve to live," he said. And he meant it, which was fucking awesome.

I grinned at him. "Oh, so you're fit to decide who should live and who shouldn't, but we're not? Who gave you the right to do that?"

I don't know what he was going to come back at me with on that one. I bet it would have been good for a laugh. But then Rachel clomped down the basement stairs, looking like she'd been eating Sweet-Tarts all day and they were starting to kick in.

"The TV," she said. "You guys better come look at this."

76

Rachel

We'd been watching *Oprah*--which I would like to state for the record was *not* my idea--when the news cut in. Some blonde bimbo in a purple suit was shuffling her papers behind the news desk, blinking owlishly and staring at the camera with no emotion at all, waiting for her cue. It's always weird when they do that on local stations. You're used to seeing those people at certain times of the day, and then they pop up suddenly, already dolled-up and dressed in their news-clothes in the middle of the afternoon, raring to go, and it sort of throws you off.

"We're getting ready to take you live to a news conference in Friedman, Illinois, where Lt. Larry Rhodes has announced that he will relay new developments in the ongoing multiple-murder cases there."

I ran to get Dave and Lucas, and they came quick.

We knew it was going to be a big deal when Rhodes came out of the wings wearing a suit-coat, instead of the short-sleeved dress shirts he usually sported on TV.

"*Lay-Ray!*" Alison cooed. "Oh my god, he has the biggest winker I've ever seen in my life!"

Four heads snapped around to look at her.

"Oh my fucking *god,*" Gretchen groaned.

"What the hell is a 'winker?'" Dave said.

Alison rolled her eyes. "I didn't *sleep* with him," she giggled. "Somebody dared him to whip it out at the Christmas party a few years ago. It had to be like this--" she held her hands up in front of her glassy eyes and moved them back and forth until she found the right distance between them--"long. And it wasn't even *hard.*"

I don't know how far apart her hands were, exactly, but if she was telling the truth, Lay-Ray was packing.

Lucas gave us a look. "Later," he said, and everybody

shut up.

Rhodes, who had been standing around like a cow waiting for somebody to take a sledgehammer to his head and put him out of his misery, finally got the go-ahead from somebody we couldn't see and stepped behind the podium.

"Good afternoon. I'm here today to announce new developments in our ongoing investigations of the multiple-murder cases here in Friedman. Last night a fire at 315 North Normal Street completely destroyed the property. This house was occupied by persons-of-interest to us in relation to the multiple-murder investigation. Surrounding properties also incurred severe damage as a result of this fire. Currently, the fire marshal is conducting an investigation to determine if arson was the cause of the fire."

"It was," Dave said. "I was there."

Gretchen giggled.

"As of this morning," Corbin continued, "two of our officers are missing. Neither Lt. Michael Reisman or Lt. David French have been seen since leaving the scene of last night's fire. Reisman and French were the officers in charge of our ongoing multiple-murder investigation. After several attempts to reach them by phone, uniformed officers were dispatched to their places of residence. No clue to their whereabouts has been found, and at this point, foul play is not suspected."

"How is that possible?" I said.

Dave grinned. "Cause we're fucking good, that's how. What I want to know is, doesn't anybody in this shitty police department rank over Lieutenant?"

Apparently the easy part was over for Rhodes--he got an expression on his face that you usually only see in commercials for Imodium A-D. "The Friedman Police Department has been stretched well beyond its means by this investigation. We've asked for help from the Federal Bureau of Investigation, and they've agreed to assist us in bringing this case to a close. I'll turn the floor over now to Special Agent Frank Hardy, who is now heading the investigation."

Dave hooted. "Holy shit! We're gonna be hunted by one of the Hardy Boys? I used to read those books all the time when I was a kid. I wonder if he's got a brother named Joe? I wonder if he knows Encyclopedia Brown, or Jupiter Jones?"

Lucas looked at him and he shut up again. But he kept grinning.

We watched the rest of it, and the wrap-up, but it didn't seem like we learned anything. At least *I* didn't learn anything. Mostly it seemed like a lot of government double-talk that was designed to make you think you were being given information when you weren't. The FBI guy answered some of the reporters questions when he was done with his little speech.

Well, they'd ask him a question and he'd say something back, anyway. I don't know that you could consider them answers, exactly.

The best part was when Todd Byrne, wearing an Action 8 baseball cap to hide his burned hair, said "Special Agent Hardy, how would you describe the general tone of the investigation at this point?"

And that FBI prick got this expression on his face that you could tell was totally practiced in the mirror every time he got done watching action movies on TV. "We're fully prepared to track the culprits of these crimes to the end of the earth, if necessary," he said. "There will be no rest for the wicked."

I thought Dave was going to wet his pants over that one.

When it was over, Lucas clapped his hands together. "Alright, listen up," he said. "We're on the clock again."

I don't know about Dave, but it sent a jolt up my spine.

"Tie 'em up. When you've got them situated, start cleaning. Everything we might have touched gets wiped down with cleanser. I want the carpets vacuumed and all trash picked up, down to the last cigarette butt. Do it fast, but do it well. When you finish with a room, turn the lights off so we know it's done."

"What about me?" Dave said. That jerk.

"You're on cleaning detail too," Lucas smirked. "Same room, same time. Two brains are better than one. If there's something you think you might need to do, do it. No margin for error here. When we leave this place, it's gonna look like nobody's been here since the owners left."

He went back to the den and left us with the girls. "Bossy asshole, isn't he?" Dave said.

"As long as it keeps some prison dyke from using my face for a bicycle seat, he can be as bossy as he wants," I said.

Dave's eyebrows went over the tops of his glasses.

"Good point. I can go my whole life without tossing a salad, and it's not gonna bother me a bit."

We got on it.

77

<u>Dave</u>

Cleaning goes against my nature. I mean, seriously, I don't see why we couldn't have just burned the place down. We'd torched our own house, and I'd actually been kind of attached to it, shithole though it was.

Fortunately, Mrs. Lucas knows more about cleaning that I ever will. She had to tell me what to do like I was a little kid, but I did it. We scrubbed that place down good, and so fast that by the time we'd finished we were both breathing hard. Our throats and noses were burning from inhaling cleansers in deep breaths for the last hour, and we felt like we needed to split a bottle of Advil and grab some serious nap-time, but we got it done. We set the trash bags by the front door, next to what passed for our luggage, and went back to the living room.

The chicks were gone.

"Ah shit!" I said, and took off running for the basement with Mrs. Lucas right behind me.

I should have known better. Those chicks hadn't gotten away--Lucas had just moved them to where the action was. Reisman's wife was laid out on another piece of plastic, still tied, in a pool of her own blood. Lucas had cut her throat from ear to ear.

"Good," he said when he saw me. "Help me wrap her before this blood gets out of hand."

"How do you wanna do it?" I said. I was kind of pissed that I wasn't going to get to see her naked, but I guess you don't get it all in one lifetime.

"Like a burrito," Luke told me. "Ends up first, then the sides." He tossed Mrs. Lucas a roll of duct tape. "Just like a Christmas present."

Halfway through, I realized that aside from crinkling plastic and the roll of duct tape squealing as Mrs. Lucas pulled pieces off of it, the room was quiet. I shot a few glances around and saw that the cops were still alive, barely, but they had gags on. Reisman was crying. Frenchie the Fridge was staring at the bundle at our feet, but he didn't look angry anymore, just hollowed out. Almost like somebody had given him a lobotomy.

The little chick had a gag on too, and she had tears running down her face, but she wasn't exactly what you'd call crying. She wasn't hitching or quivering or anything. Very odd. I have to give her credit--she might have been a trashy little slut, but she was cold-blooded. It was kind of hot, in a sleazy, dangerous sort of way.

When we got her mom taped up to Lucas' satisfaction, he looked at the little chick. She looked right back at him. "Is that still what you want?" he asked her, and that was weird, too--I don't think I'd ever heard him talk to anybody that gently, whatever he was talking about. Coming from him, on top of all that cleanser we'd inhaled, it was disorienting.

Vampira closed her eyes and nodded. Lucas put a hand on her forehead to brace her and pulled the tape off her mouth. "This is it," he said. "If you've got something to say, say it now."

You could tell she was working on it in her head-- whatever she was going to say, she wanted to get it right. And Lucas looked like he was going to give her the time to do it. Within reason, of course. I'm not sure what was dictating our schedule, but it seemed like we were in a bit of a hurry.

Luke ripped the tape off Reisman's mouth and watched him gasp for air. "You fucking son-of-a-bitch," Reisman sobbed. "You dirty lowdown fucking son-of-a-bitch. I hope I go to hell so I can be waiting for you when you get there. One way or another, I'm gonna make you pay for this."

"Good luck with that," Lucas nodded. "I'll be rooting for you. But you ain't dead yet, hoss. We've still got business to do."

"What?" Reisman screamed. *"I've told you everything I know. I watched you kill my wife! What more do you think I have to give you?"*

"Nothing," Lucas said. "You're useless to me now. But I had a talk with your girl awhile ago, and she wants something. I'm inclined to give it to her."

To say that Reisman looked confused wouldn't begin to touch it. We might as well have all started speaking French and belly-bucking each other like sumo wrestlers.

"She wants to watch you die," Lucas told him. "Any idea why that might be?

"Oh God, Gretchen, why?" he wailed. *"Gretchen, no!"*

Lucas turned to the girl. "This is your shining moment, kid. Whatever you've got, you better give it up."

I looked at Rachel, and she nodded back at me with wide eyes.

Lucas cut the kid loose, hands, feet and all. "Go on," he said, and patted her on the shoulder.

Nothing happened for a few seconds. I guess the kid had stage fright or something. She kept looking around the room at us, like we were supposed to start feeding her lines. I was two seconds from making fun of her when she went into action.

"I hate you," she said. She jumped up out of her folding chair like she meant to lunge at her dad, but once she was on her feet she just sort of stood there, wavering. "I hate your fucking *guts.*"

She stared Lucas in the eye. "I've changed my mind," she said. "I can't kill him. But I can kill Frenchie, if you let me."

Lucas mulled it over and lit a cigarette.

"Three years ago, when I was like, twelve?" she said. "I started filling out. I got these big tits almost overnight. Guys started looking at me different. I knew what they wanted. I'm not stupid.

"So this kid who lived down the block, Jason Gholson, he was like a freshman, was always asking me if he could play with them. He didn't want to fuck me, he just wanted to touch my boobs. He wasn't rude about it or anything. He just really likes tits. So I was sort of curious about it, and he kept asking, and one day I was on my way back from the pool, and I saw him riding his bike around. And he asked me again, and I let him."

She paused, like she was waiting for some sort of reaction from Lucas, but he didn't say anything. Big surprise, I know.

"We couldn't do it on the street, out in the open, so we went back to my house," she said. "In the garage, with the door closed. Nobody was home. We started kissing a little bit, and I took the top of my swimsuit down, and he started playing with them. Just touching them at first. It felt really good. And he asked me if he could suck on them, and I said yeah. And that felt even better."

"Gretchen," Reisman groaned. "Stop it. Don't do this."

"Shut up!" she yelled. *"Shut your fucking mouth!"*

She looked at Lucas. "It wasn't anything dirty. I swear it wasn't. I wasn't going to let him fuck me. He didn't even ask. It was like, a kid thing, you know? But then my dad and Frenchie came home to get something, and they came in the back door of the garage, and there I am, with this horny high school kid sucking my nipples. And they freaked out. My dad hit Jason in the head, and Frenchie started kicking him in the ass. I got in big trouble over that one. And Jason never talked to me again."

Lucas offered her his cigarette and she took a drag. It didn't go down too smooth, but you could tell it wasn't her first.

"A couple months later, we go out for this camping trip. Me and my dad, Frenchie and a couple of his sister's kids. I

172

sort of knew them. They were like in high school, so I wasn't around them all the time. But I knew they were fucking assholes, just like Frenchie. Bullies. And they were both staring at me from the time I got to the cabin. It was still warm enough to swim, and everybody was going into the lake, but I didn't want to. Cause I knew that those two would just be eyeballing my tits the whole time, making their disgusting comments and wading around with boners."

She gave me a look that might have been a little dirty, but it didn't last long enough for me to be sure. Whatever she was selling, she was selling it to Lucas.

"But my dad *made* me swim. He told me he was sick of me being a pain in the ass, and that I needed to get with the program. I was ruining everybody's good time. So I did it. I stayed away from them, but I got in my suit and splashed around in the lake long enough to make him happy. We were supposed to be having like some kind of cheesy bonding time, to make up for all the times he treated me like shit, or something. But all he did was suck down beers and tell a bunch of trucker jokes with the guys."

I didn't know where this story was going, but I had a pretty good idea. And I didn't like it. Call me a hypocritical bastard if you wanna, but it was starting to make me feel sick. Four horny guys, alone in the woods with alcohol and a busty 12 year-old in a swimsuit? They don't make any Disney movies like that. At least none that I've ever seen.

Vampira was starting to shake. Lucas handed her the half of his cigarette that was left and lit another. He was crouched down at that point, which is apparently some weird thing that people with rural, automotive upbringings do. Sort of like cowboys around a campfire in one of those Clint Eastwood movies, right before the shit hits the fan. I've tried doing it a couple of times, but I always get charley-horses behind my knees and have to keep putting my hands on the floor to steady myself, which sort of makes it impossible to look and feel cool and therefore defeats the whole purpose. For me, anyway.

"Gretchen--" Reisman started, but Lucas stared at him, and he stopped. "She *lies,*" he said. "She lies all the time. You can't believe anything she says. She's sick."

Lucas' eyes were brown ice. "Quiet."

"But--"

Lucas pointed the knife at him. "It's not a debate."

Reisman dropped his chin. "Go on," Lucas said. He reached out and gave Vampira a reassuring pat on the back of her thigh. "You're doing fine."

She coughed into her fist and looked over at Rachel and I. We nodded at her.

"We went back to the cabin and started cooking stuff for supper. Those assholes Frenchie brought with him asked if they could have some beers, and they let them. All of them started getting loud and obnoxious, even for them. We were just getting ready to eat when my dad got a call on his cell phone. Somebody from the cop shop needed him to come back to town and do something, I don't know what. I asked if I could go with him, cause I didn't want to be left alone with those assholes. I just wanted to go home. But he said he'd be back by morning. We were supposed to go fishing. I told him I didn't care about fishing, I don't even *like* fishing. I just wanted to go home. But he said no. My mom was in Chicago for the weekend, and he wasn't going to leave me home alone. *'I know what kind of shit you get up to when you're home alone,'* he said, and him and Frenchie started laughing.

"As soon as he was gone, Frenchie started telling his nephews about the time they came home and caught me and Jason in the garage. They all thought that was hilarious. Then one of them said I should give them a demonstration. *'I can't picture it,'* one of them said. *'I think I'm gonna need a visual aid.'*"

Her cigarette was almost spent, and she looked around for a place to put it. Frenchie was glaring at her. "Fuck you," she sneered, and flicked it at him. It bounced off his chest and landed on his crotch. We watched him wiggle around like a jackass until he got it off and it hissed in the bloody liquid on the tarp under his chair.

"They raped me," she said, and tears started rolling down her face. "All three of them. There was a bunch more talking, but... they took turns holding me down. They broke my cherry. They fucked me in the mouth and in the ass. They fucked my tits and bit them. They came all over my face and made me lick it up. They scooped bloody come out of my *asshole* and made me lick it off their fingers. Then they all got hard and did it again. I couldn't sit right for a week after that. Every time I went to the bathroom, I shit blood."

"That's a lie!" Reisman yelled. "I don't know why you're making this shit up now, but stop it."

"I'm not making it up!" she screamed. It was a good one, too--she leaned forward from the waist and did it so hard her voice broke. And then she was *really* crying. It made me nauseous to look at her, and Rachel said later that she felt the same way. Pain and misery rolling off her in waves that you could almost taste, and we had to just stand there. There was nothing we could do about it, nothing any of us could do to make it go away.

And the fucked-up thing is, I wanted to. I really did. All the horrible shit I've seen and done, but watching that kid freak out made me want to crawl right out of my skin and burn it so I'd never have to get back into it.

"He *said* you wouldn't believe me," Vampira said, her breath stuttering in her chest. "You know what he told me? *'Your old man knows you're a dirty lying* slut. *He told me all about it, a bunch of times. So who's he gonna believe? A filthy little* whore *who lets zit-faced kids suck her titties in a dirty garage, or his partner?'*"

"Oh Jesus," Reisman groaned, and we all knew he'd said it, or at least something like it. "I'm so sorry," he said. "Baby girl, I'm so sorry. I didn't know."

"You didn't *want* to know," she said. "Nobody wants to know. At least not the way it really happened. But when those assholes his went back to school, they told *everybody*. They left out the part about them holding me down. The part about them *raping* me. They told everybody who would listen that I was a nasty little slut who loves sucking cock and taking it up the ass. They said I *beg* for it.

"You know what that's like? To go to school every day and have people staring at you, thinking you're a whore? Girls don't wanna talk to you. I don't have any friends. And every horny guy in the place looking you over all the time, making blow-job faces at you, trying to get you to fuck them in the weight room? Grabbing your ass and feeling you up in the hallways? Even some of the teachers. *'Oh, you're gonna fail English unless you come over to my house Thursday night and do some* extra credit *work. Don't worry, I've heard all about you. It won't be anything you haven't done before, right? Just make sure you come to the back door, and don't knock before my wife leaves.'"*

Rachel smacked me on the arm, and for a second it confused me. I was just standing there, but I was so wrapped up in the story that for a second I thought maybe I'd done something wrong by accident. But she wasn't even looking at me. She was staring at Vampira, who was staring at the two worthless pieces of shit tied to the dining room chairs. And she had snake-eyes. Lucas-eyes. They weren't the same, not exactly, but they were close. If somebody had taken pictures of their faces, cropped out everything but the eyes and laid them side-by-side, you would have sworn they were related.

"You wanna know what happens?" Vampira said. She was starting to smile--with both sides of her mouth, thank God, or I would have totally freaked out. It was still too close to one of Luke's nasty smiles for my comfort. "You wanna know what happens when everybody thinks you're a whore?"

"Gretchen, I don't think you're a who--"

"*Liar,*" she said. "I've heard you, motherfucker. I've heard about the things you've told other people, trying to get a laugh, trying to make everybody like you. I've heard it come straight out of your own mouth. Remember the last time you took me to that bullshit group home? *'She's turning out to be a damn whore, and I'm sick of it.'* That's what you told the doctor, right in front of me. And you know what? You were right. I have been a whore. When people think you're shit, you start to believe it. Nobody my own age wants anything to do with me that doesn't involve me fucking them like a porno slut. Guys always wanna fuck, don't they? And if they want to give me rides and buy me clothes and get me high and give me money, and all I have to do is what everybody already says I do anyway, why not? It's not like I've got anything left to lose."

Yikes.

I didn't necessarily agree with the logic there, but I could sort of understand where it was coming from. Especially from an emotionally vulnerable teenage girl.

Rachel cleared her throat. "Didn't you try to tell your mom?" she said. "I mean, wouldn't she have done something?"

Vampira looked down at the bundle on the floor. "You couldn't tell her anything," she said. "All she ever gave a shit about was how you looked when you left the house and how many pills she had left before her prescription ran out."

Then she whirled around and booted the end of the

package where her mom's head was, as hard as she could. She almost lost her balance and fell over, but she kept it together. Fortunately, the plastic kept it together too. A bag of bloody death with a leak in it is nobody's friend.

"Useless pill-head fucking *bitch*," Vampira grunted. "She fucked around, you know. She wouldn't admit it, but I knew. Maybe I've had a lot of dicks, but at least I never lied about it. I never put up some everything's-alright front and tried to pretend I had all this class and dignity. All she ever cared about was how shit looked to everybody else. New clothes and new cars and where we were going on vacation. Anything else was your tough shit. She didn't want to hear about it."

Anybody else feel like singing "Janie's Got a Gun?" I know I do.

Let's be honest--no matter what's going on, my brain always comes back to how it affects me. Shallow, I know, but what are you gonna do? And that was when I started wondering if it was gonna get even more cramped in the back of that goddamn Camaro. I've never been sure how Lucas thinks about anything, exactly, but Vampira was beginning to look like a pledge with potential for our little glee club.

I didn't like it. We already had one high-maintenance vagina in the gang, and that was almost too much. Plus, this chick was still a kid. At least Mrs. Lucas was an adult when we picked her up. We weren't gonna have to worry about enrolling her in school, or about getting caught taking her over state lines. She was already mature.

At least as mature as I am, anyway, which is just enough to get by.

Vampira, on the other hand, was probably still young enough to get really excited about horsies, whichever side of them she wanted to ride on.

"That's it," she sighed. "I don't have anything else to say."

Lucas stood up in one effortless motion and looked at Reisman. His buck knife was open and ready in his hand.

"Wait," Reisman said. *"Wait!"*

Lucas didn't.

He grabbed the cop by the hair on top of his head and plunged the blade into the side of his throat, straight through the jugular. Reisman let out a scream that only lasted a second, until Luke twisted his wrist and severed the vocal cords. After that it was nothing but twitches and spurts.

"Ah Luke," Rachel said. "What if he was going to apologize?"

"Apologies won't undo anything he's done," he said, and looked at Vampira. "Will they?"

The chick was hypnotized by the waves of blood running down her old man's chest and staining the crotch of his boxer shorts. "No," she said. It was almost a whisper.

Watching somebody die from a throat-shot can seem like it takes a long time when you're in the moment, but it's not really all that long. A couple of minutes, tops. The thing that impressed me most was that Luke managed to do it without getting anything on him. If it had been me, I'd have looked like a used tampon.

Luke pulled the knife out of Reisman's neck and wiped it clean on his shellacked hair. The scent of blood in the air had an undercurrent of urine in it. A few seconds later it was joined by the unmistakable smell of shit, but I knew it would get a whole lot worse when we had to move the body. "Ugly, isn't it?"

"Yeah," Vampira nodded. She crinkled her nose. "Does that... I mean, you know, every time?"

"Nothing's every time," Lucas told her. "Constant variations on a theme, you might say."

"Oh."

"Man, I hope you've been eating your Wheaties," I said to Lucas. "If we have to wrap those assholes in the same sheet of plastic and haul them out of here, one of us is liable to drop a nut."

"It'll be alright," he said.

Vampira giggled.

"You're up," Luke told her, and held the knife out to her handle-first.

She looked at it, but didn't reach for it. "Really?" she said. "You're really gonna let me do it?"

"If you want to."

"Yeah," she said. "But I mean, you know, how do I do it? What's the best way?"

"Any way you want," he said. "It's your deal."

"It's not that hard," I told her. "Bodies want to die, they just need a reason."

She looked around at each of us and stepped back from

Frenchie, waving us toward her. And we went. "I kind of have an idea, but I don't know if it's any good," she whispered. "I've thought about killing him a bunch of times, but that was just thinking, you know?"

Jesus Christ. How fucking hard is it to off somebody? I mean, he was already half-dead anyway. It's not like we have to stand around and whisper about it like some practical joke we're about to pull on him.

If you want to over-dramatize and over-think something, just throw a teenage girl into the mix. They'll weigh you down like an anchor every time.

"I want to cut it off," Vampira said. "Is that cool?"

That'll put a grimace on a guy's face, let me tell you. I'd never even thought about doing that, and up to that point, I assumed I'd gone through almost everything. I guess my professors were right--arrogance and self-satisfaction really are the downfall of every artist.

"Won't that be really, really messy?" Mrs. Lucas asked. "I mean, it is just one big vein, more or less."

She had a point. We'd never done it, but I was pretty sure it would involve maximum clean-up. Lucas had made me and Pete watch this movie called *I Spit On Your Grave* one time, where this city chick got raped by rednecks over and over again for half an hour, and then she takes her revenge. She'd gotten one of the guys into a bathtub, telling him that she'd liked being raped by him, which he believed, because he was a redneck and a rapist.

Not exactly the top of the intellectual food-chain, that guy.

But anyway, he went for it, and then she went for it, and he ended up spurting blood like a hose all over her bathroom. It was almost as bad to watch as the rape itself.

"Probably won't be as messy if he's not hard," Lucas shrugged, "but it's still gonna be rough."

"You've already got plastic laid out," Vampira said. I didn't know her that well, but it felt like she might be working herself into a pout. "But, you know, whatever. I don't care."

Luke and I looked at each other; I moved my eyes back and forth like a head-shake to throw in my vote. He was impossible to read, as always. Stone-faced bastard.

"What if I take my clothes off?" Vampira offered.

I don't think anybody knew what that was supposed to add to the equation, but it sure piqued my interest. She was kind of odd to look at when you first laid eyes on her, but the longer you were around her, the hotter she got.

"You know, so I don't get any on me," she said.

One side of Luke's mouth went back. "Whatever you want," he said. "Knock yourself out."

78

Rachel

I couldn't *believe* that Lucas told that girl she could get naked to kill somebody. I mean, okay, she wanted to--rape victim or not, that kid was a fucking *slut*. Little Miss Teenage Wet Dream. After hearing her story, I'd assumed it was just an image she projected, some sort of psychological defense to deal with the trauma. I figured it was at least 80% bullshit.

Apparently, I was wrong.

Nobody in the room knew for sure what was going on but Lucas, and as usual, he wasn't telling anybody. Even Dave looked shocked when Gretchen yanked her TOOL shirt over her head and her boobs were staring at us. And I have to admit, it was some set. They looked so big and high under her shirt that I had just assumed she was wearing some kind of push-up bra. No such luck. They hung that way all on their lonesome.

For all the ladies out there--if you ever want to come within a fraction of throwing yourself off an emotional ledge, try having the guy you have a huge crush on tell a curvy teenage girl to get naked in front of you while you're fresh off a miscarriage, packing cotton, and generally feel more unattractive than you've ever felt in your life.

The Doc Martens came off next, then the socks. When she dropped her pants and was standing there in front of us in just a thong, I thought Dave was gonna choke on his gum.

"Somebody pinch me," he muttered. "Quick."

I slapped him in the back of the head.

"Close enough," he said. Not that he bothered to look at me.

Then she bent over, peeled off the thong, and we got a clear view of her nether region, which was bald as a newborn babe. "Holy lola," Dave said. "You shave your asshole? I mean, you know, yourself?"

"Sure," Gretchen grinned. "Pretty hot, huh?"

"How do you *do* that?" he said. "I cut myself shaving my face, and it's in plain sight and easy to reach."

She shrugged, those big tits of hers covered with goosebumps and jiggling like twin Jell-O molds fresh from the fridge. "Practice makes perfect," she said. "You just have to take your time and have a really good mirror."

"Sure," Dave nodded. He looked at me and winced. "Is it me, or have I just reached a state of total retardation?"

"You have," I said. "But it's not just you."

Lucas wasn't even looking at our Lolita--he was watching Frenchie, who was staring at her hard enough with one eye to make up for what the other one was missing. And pitching a nice little tent in his whitey-tighties, I might add.

Dave noticed it too. "Oh yeah," he said. "This is gonna be a mess, alright."

Gretchen padded back and forth on the carpet, gently circling her belly-button with her fingertips. "I look pretty good, huh?" she smiled at Frenchie. "Better than the last time you saw me like this?"

Frenchie grunted something behind the duct tape. I don't know what it was, but it didn't exactly sound like disagreement.

She giggled. "I bet you remember that night pretty good, don't you?" she said. "Do you think about it a lot? Because I do. All the time."

Frenchie nodded. It almost seemed involuntary. The hair on his chest was matted with blood and who-knows-what; the skin beneath was beginning to flush. The wood of the dining room chair he was tied to began to creak and groan as he strained against the ropes. He did not look like a happy camper. In fact, he looked like he would have choked her to death with his bare hands. Probably while raping her again.

Lucas was scraping something under the nail on his index finger with the tip of the buck knife's blade. We made eye-contact and he winked at me. He seemed incredibly bored by the whole thing.

Dave was staring at Gretchen's ass like he was trying to mentally separate her cheeks and get another look at her clean-shaven little butthole. Lucas glanced at him and back at me, silently chuckling as both sides of his mouth went back.

"How's it going there, Davey?" he said. "You look like you're wound for sound."

"I'm wound for *something*," Dave replied. He managed to tear his eyes away from his amateur proctology long enough to grin at us.

It's not that I held it against him--if I was a guy, I probably would have been staring at her too. But it was still uncomfortable to witness. Taken out of a very specific context, male lust always makes me really, really ill at ease. It's ugly and it's dangerous. The realization that men are driven by something so unstable and potentially volatile doesn't exactly fill you with a sense of safety, you know? And since I'd already seen first-hand some of the things Dave considered a good time, the whole thing was starting to creep me out in a major way.

Gretchen was talking to Frenchie the whole time, but I can't remember what she was saying. I was having a little trouble concentrating on the business at hand. Whatever it was, she seemed to be getting more and more animated as she said it. And Frenchie was right there with her. It sounded like the chair was about to fly apart at any moment.

Gretchen fell to her knees on the plastic in front of him with a with a squishing sound, little splashes of pink liquid shooting up on her calves and lower thighs. It looked like it would hurt--there was nothing under the tarp but cold concrete floor--but if it did, she ignored it.

"Let's see what you've got going on down here *now*," she said, and hooked her fingers into the waistband of his underwear, yanking it back until it ripped and exposed him to the room, his Mr. Mister swollen and stabbing the air in front of her face. She slapped at it like a bobble-head doll at watched it move from side to side before coming to rest where it had started--pointing right at her chin.

"Wow," she said. "It's a lot smaller than I remembered it, Frenchie. Of course, the last time I saw it, I didn't have much to compare it to, did I?"

I sidled up to Lucas and wrapped my arms around his bicep. The clothes he wore were deceiving--he was solid as a rock underneath them. Right up close to him like that, he seemed impossibly big. The top of my head barely cleared his shoulder. "I don't like this," I murmured in the direction of his ear.

"I know you don't," he said. He turned his wrist and

laid a hand on my hip, giving it a squeeze that made my stomach flutter. He left the hand where it was, palming me like a basketball, almost as if he was shielding me from something. "Hang in there for me, kid. We're almost done."

He gave the buck knife an underhand toss and managed to drop it with a *thunk* on a clean spot of plastic within Gretchen's reach. She stared at it for a second and then turned her head toward us.

"Do it, if you're gonna," Lucas said. "You're gonna fuck around and lose your nerve."

She leaned over and picked it up, hefting it in her hand. "The only one here who's gonna lose anything is *him*," she said. She cupped her left hand under Frenchie's balls and jiggled them, his hard-on beginning to wilt as he tried to yell something behind the gag.

"Your buddies are gonna find you with your cock in your mouth. We'll see how great they think you are *then*, huh?" she sneered, and pulled his testicles up and out, sliding the knife edge under them. *"Rape-o motherfucker."*

When she started sawing away at him the gag wasn't enough to muffle the screams, not completely. His balls came off in her hand and she dropped them between his feet, switching her grip to his now-limp penis as she began to cut the bottom of it. Blood flew. It hit her neck and chest and rolled down in tiny-bubbled waves, coating her big jiggling boobs like paint, drops flicking off to either side of her as she put extra effort into it.

"Jesus *Christ*," Dave groaned. He had his hands in front

of his crotch and looked like he was about to be sick.

I wanted to look away, but I couldn't. I'm not sure why. Sometimes you just have to know, I guess.

Gretchen sat back on her haunches, her chest heaving up and down as she tried to catch her breath. "I can't get it," she gasped. "It's like part of it won't cut or something."

"Didn't figure it would," Lucas said. "Probably should have used a camp-saw."

The blood flow was less urgent now--the stuff was more or less falling out of Frenchie in lazy, irregular splatters as his heart stopped beating. The vessels in his one open eye were blown, the white that circled his glassy brown iris now mostly red.

"That sucks," Gretchen sighed. "I wanted to get it all the way off."

She couldn't have been too disappointed--her nipples were poking through the sheen of blood on her chest like pencil erasers. I pressed my forehead into Lucas' warm shoulder and tried to ignore the taste in my mouth. I felt like I was going to be sick.

79

<u>Dave</u>

Big-titted naked chicks covered in blood are totally hot. I'm not even kidding about that.

That chick had blood all over her, too--with no pubes to slow it down it was even dripping over her snowflake. When she stood up and arched her back to get the kinks out she left two bloody handprints on the top of her ass. "That was *awesome!*" she grinned. "Was it cool? I mean, you know, did I do it right and everything?"

"He's dead," I shrugged. "It doesn't get much righter than that."

She shifted her weight from foot to foot, making the plastic crinkle and squish. "Man, you guys were right, I'm a mess," she said. "I didn't know that blood smelled so bad. Kind of like rotten pennies."

She was trying to play it off like it was no big deal, but I've been there. The first one sends you in twenty different directions at once, because there's a moment where it sinks in that the whole thing is for real, and you can't undo it. It plays out in your skull like a shitty rock video, or maybe a commercial where some jackass who didn't know what he was doing tries to slip you subliminal messages but leaves them running for a few frames too long. It's all overlapping layers that are slightly out of sync, some of them bleeding through the mix with more urgency than the others. A sort of highlight reel of what you've just done, and you can't shut it off.

You might want to get off that ride, but you can't. You're in the car, the bar is locked down over your lap, and you can either piss your pants or throw your arms up and scream till you think your throat will burst. Think Slim Pickens riding the bomb in *Dr. Strangelove,* but for real.

"What do we do now?" I said, because somebody had to say *something.* I wondered what happened to our timeframe, which had apparently been thrown right out the goddamn window. At the rate we were moving, we were gonna be there when the owners came back next summer.

"Two ideas," Luke said. "But both of them are pretty labor-intensive."

"Great," I deadpanned. "I love labor."

"We can bury them, or we can lake them," he said.

Mrs. Lucas, who was clinging to him like he was a big scary teddy bear, looked up. "Won't they float up after a while if we put them in the water?"

"If we split their stomachs open and shovel some sand in there before we wrap them, it might keep the gas from building up," he shrugged. "I don't know. I've never tried it."

"We could cut a few slits in the plastic," I said. "That would let the water in and the gas out."

Lucas gave me a one-sided grin. "Good idea."

It sounded like a lot of work, but it sounded like less work than digging a big-ass hole and filling it up again. "Have they got a boat laying around here somewhere?" I asked. "We don't want to do it right by the shore, do we?"

"There's a float platform tied to the dock back there," he said. "It's better. No motor noise. We'll have to hunt up a couple of paddles, though. They're probably either down here or in the garage."

We were gearing up to go into full *A-Team* mode, which is always awesome. Then Vampira killed the whole vibe.

"*Ah-hem,*" she said. "I guess you guys have forgotten than I'm standing here naked and covered in fucking *blood.*"

"It's not that we've forgotten," I told her. "It's just that nobody gives a shit."

"Well what am I supposed to do?" she said. Her voice was on the outskirts of whiney and moving fast. "This stuff smells bad. And it's starting to get sticky."

Rachel rolled her eyes and grabbed a bucket that was underneath the wash-sink. She dropped it into the basin with a clatter and started filling it. The best part was, she didn't bother to rinse it out first, so there were cobwebs and a couple of dead bugs floating around in it.

"What's *your* fucking problem?" Vampira said.

Mrs. Lucas' eyes narrowed. "You're a pain in the ass," she said. *"That's* my fucking problem."

She took the bucket out of the sink and set it down on the tarp hard enough to make water splash over the top. Then she grabbed an old dried-up yellow sponge that has one of those green scratch pads on the other side and threw it at her. It was a good shot too--it nicked a little clean patch in the blood that was drying on Vampira's stomach. "Sorry we don't have any bubble bath or rubber ducks for you. Try to make the best of it."

Lucas actually laughed out loud at that.

"Fucking *bitch,*" Vampira spat. She knelt down to pick up the sponge and noticed the bugs floating in the top of the bucket. "I'm not using this. It's fucking disgusting."

He's never come right out and said so, but I've always gotten the impression that Lucas doesn't like it when girls swear excessively. He doesn't seem to mind the occasional four-letter word thrown in for emphasis, but when "fuck" is a chick's main adjective and adverb, I think it sort of irritates him. Me too, for that matter. I don't have any hang-ups about girls being particularly ladylike or anything. I just don't think they're any good at swearing. It doesn't flow naturally. They put the wrong emphasis on the words, and it always sounds like they're trying to show off.

"Let's go," Lucas told her. He wasn't smiling any more. "We've got things to do."

Vampira gave him a dirty look, but she dunked the sponge in the bucket and started wiping herself off. At first it seemed like she was trying to put on a little performance, but when she realized that nobody really gave a shit she gave up and started doing it like she meant it. Lucas grabbed a broom that was leaning in the corner by the water heater and started sweeping up all the cigarette butts we'd dropped on the floor. There were a lot of them.

"You got the upstairs all squared away," he said.

Mrs. Lucas nodded. "It looks good. All the lights are off, the beds are made, and our stuff is by the front door. As soon as we get this taken care of, we're out of here."

Something about the way she said *this* gave me the impression that she wasn't just talking about the three bodies we already had. Or at least she hoped she wasn't. No one had said anything about what we were going to do with Vampira, but I was ready to give her the thumbs-down as soon as anybody asked. Yeah she was hot, and yeah my penis had a few ambitious ideas, but my brain had it outvoted 47-to-1.

Lucas changed his grip on the broom and swept the mess into a dustpan. "Don't let me forget that," he said.

"We'll toss it in the water with the rest of it."

Vampira finished cleaning herself and dropped the sponge-scrubber in the bucket, where the water had turned pink. She was shivering. "No towel, I guess," she said. Her nipples were pink rocks on the ends of her tits.

Watching her get back into her clothes wasn't nearly as much fun as watching her get out of them. Although I did get to take another look at her holes when she bent over to grab her underwear, so it wasn't a total loss. I remember thinking that it was too bad she had such a shit personality. If it wasn't for that, she would have been really hot.

Lucas picked up his buck knife and began wiping it down with the same rag he'd been using all day. He was taking his time, making sure he got everything out of all the nooks and crannies. A breeze had been picking up outside, and when it died down for a second, we could hear the furnace kick on. It was the only sound in the basement.

80

Rachel

Those two cops were a mess. Reisman had managed to lose control of his bowels, which didn't exactly add anything to the situation, and there was a lot of loose liquid rolling around on the tarp. Even with the blood mixed in there to stiffen it up, it was still nasty.

Lucas and Dave cut them loose and flopped them down face-first on the tarp, sending another waft of stench into the cold basement air. "I don't think this is gonna work," Dave said. "Even if we wrap them up, we still gotta get them up the stairs. If we drag them, won't the tarp get a hole in it and leak all that crap out?"

Lucas made a face and nodded. "We're gonna have to piece them out." He took another look around the basement. "There's a whole box of black garbage bags down here somewhere, and we're gonna need a couple of saws. Preferably hacksaws."

"Well, so much for the easy way out," Dave said. "Think it'll actually work?"

Lucas grinned. "It's gotta work better than you and your bad ribs trying to buck them out of here whole."

"Touché," Dave said. "You big sweetie, you."

They went to work on that while we girls watched. "So am I like, in the gang now?" Gretchen murmured to me. "I mean, you know, is there like, other stuff I gotta do?"

The earnestness on her face was both irritating and sad. "I'm not really in charge of that," I told her, careful to keep any trace of bitchiness out of my voice. "I'm sort of the low-man on the totem pole here."

"But you want me, right?" she said. "I mean, I know we've been kind of fighting a little bit, but no hard feelings or anything?"

I shook my head. "No hard feelings."

I don't know if I was lying or not.

She sighed. "That's cool. I don't want you being like, mad at me, or anything. You seem like a really awesome chick. I never had a friend like you before."

Ah *Jesus*.

You have to give her credit--that little tramp really knew how to put the emotional screws to you, whether that was her intention or not. Once you got past that hard-candy shell of hers she was pink and raw inside, just desperate for somebody to want her around. It made you want to hug her.

"We can talk about it later," I said, and put my hand in the small of her back. "Right now, we've got other stuff we have to deal with first, okay?"

"Sure!" she grinned, and then lowered her voice to a stage-whisper. "I mean, sure, okay."

We watched them work. "Should we be helping them or something?" she frowned.

"Nah," I said. "They know what they're doing."

81

Dave

If anybody ever asks you to help them cut up three bodies, bag the parts, shovel some sand in the bags and then chuck them into a lake, my advice would be to run like the dickens. It's not a lot of fun, especially if you've got bad ribs and it feels like you're being kicked by a mule every time you lift or throw something.

We double-bagged the hands, feet, and heads and threw them in the trunk of the Camaro so we could chuck them off the bridge into the Mississippi River on our way to wherever we were going. The rest of it went into the deep part of Lake Suede, along with the filing cabinet and most of the files. Lucas did all of the rowing and most of the throwing, because he's a go-getter. The chicks stayed back on the shore.

"What are we gonna do with the last one?" I said after we'd chucked the last of the bags in and started back. "We're not taking her with us, are we?"

It was cloudy that night, no moon, but I could still make out his silhouette as he paddled. "We need her for a little bit," he said. "Maybe another couple of hours."

I didn't know what we needed her *for*, but I was willing to wait it out. Mostly I just wanted to crawl into the backseat of the Camaro and fall asleep for a week. "Good," I said. "If we keep picking people up, we're gonna have to trade in your Batmobile and buy a mini-van."

Lucas spat into the water. "I can't let you have this one," he told me. "I'm working on something, and that might trash the whole deal."

"That's okay," I said. "I'm wiped. Plus, that chick sort of freaks me out."

"How so?"

"I'm not really into the idea of cold-dating an admitted whore," I said. "Kind of a turn-off, right there."

"I saw you checking her out."

"She's hot," I nodded, which was pointless since he probably couldn't see me anyway. "But the germ-factor's too much for me. If you're gonna do that, you might as well hump a porta-potty."

The wind that whipped across the surface of the lake was cold. It cut right through my sweatshirt and made my loose teeth chatter. Somewhere underneath it you could hear the sound of the paddle moving through the water, steering us closer to the shore.

I think Lucas was a little irritated at having to change plans in mid-stream. Reisman's wife had already been bagged up, which meant we had to unwrap her to take her apart. The whole deal took longer than it would have if I'd been 100% or we'd had better tools, and we'd reached the point where every minute that went by seemed like it was putting us that much closer to being caught. That was a heavy weight to have pressing down on you. Especially when the heat of the moment had passed and the possibility of jail was as real as it ever got.

"I'm starting to get a little nervous," I said. I felt like an asshole, but at least my teeth stopped clacking together for a couple of seconds. "I mean, I didn't think this was gonna take this long, did you?"

"No."

Funny how it never struck me until that moment that Lucas does the majority of his talking with his eyes. The inflections in his voice don't change all that much. With him, there are a hundred variations on the word "no," and all of them mean something different. But since I couldn't see his face, I had no idea which one of them he was using. It did nothing to brace my confidence.

"Shit," I said.

He took pity on me, the bastard. "The FBI is nothing to fuck around with," he said. "They know how to do shit these local boys could never even dream of. I knew they'd be coming, but I wasn't planning on cutting it this close."

"Level with me," I told him. "Just how fucked are we, exactly?"

He seemed to think about it. I could tell by his silhouette that he was looking at the back of the house as we approached. "Fucked enough, I suppose," he said. "We gotta get a lot of miles between us and here before we can relax. We're gonna have to be careful and run like hell at the same time."

I didn't have to say it, but I wanted to. "I've got your back, no matter what," I said. "You know that, right?"

We were almost to the dock. "Never doubted it," he said.

It sounded like he was grinning.

82

Rachel

We took back roads that got worse before they got better, but eventually we were back on a highway of some kind. How Lucas knew where he was going, I have no idea. I've got a pretty fair sense of direction, but we twisted and turned and doubled-back so many times that I couldn't have told you which way was up if you held a gun to my head. In the dark there weren't even any landmarks out there--it was all just old barns and farmhouses that sat far back from the road, with an occasional rusting trailer that looked like a meth-lab waiting to happen. Inside the car it was quiet. Lucas had turned the radio off, and if anybody had anything to say, they were keeping it to themselves.

We pulled into some no-horse town near the Iowa state line at 11:37, according to the digital clock on the sign for the Farmers' Bank of Wherever. The rest of us were drowsy, but Lucas was checking out everything the way only Lucas can. We cruised up the main drag once and then went to the side streets, angling around until he found an alley he liked and pulled in. He killed the headlights but left the car running.

"Gretchen," he said. "You asleep back there?"

"Almost," she yawned.

"Wake it up there, kid. I need you to do something."

She sat up straight. "Okay."

"You know how to use an ATM machine?"

"Yeah," she said. "I mean, I've never done it, but I think so."

Lucas pulled a credit card out of the pocket of his hoodie and passed it back to her. "There's one in the side of that bank over there. You should be able to get $500."

She looked at the card. "Won't I need a number? Like a code, or something?"

"2668," he said, and made her repeat it back to him. "Quick as you can, but take it easy. No running."

He opened the door and got out, holding one finger on the metal button inside the door jamb to keep the interior light off as he leaned the seat forward. She crawled out of the backseat and looked at him. "2268," she said. "Got it."

He climbed back in and stuck the toe of his boot on the button, lighting a cigarette. "Who's card?" I asked.

"Her dad's."

It made sense--when they couldn't find Reisman or Frenchie, they'd start checking their bank transactions. And if there was a surveillance camera anywhere around the ATM, all they'd see was Reisman's darling daughter, taking out a large amount of cash with her daddy's card.

"How'd you get the number?" I said.

From the darkness of the backseat I could hear Dave giggle.

"Okay," I said. "Ask a stupid question... but how do you know he gave you the right one?"

"Don't know for sure," Lucas said. "He gave me a couple different ones to begin with. But that was the one he stuck with when the pain started getting bad."

"You missed your calling in life," I told him. "You should have worked for CIA."

"Thought about it," he said. "Too much suit-and-tie action for me."

Now *there's* an image I'd never thought of--Lucas in a tie. Black, of course. He'd probably look like the lost Blues Brother.

I was expecting a long, torturous wait, but Gretchen came back after only a quick couple of minutes, digging a wad of $20s out of her pocket. "I think we might be in trouble," she said. "I'm pretty sure nobody saw me, but there's a couple of cop cars parked down the street."

Lucas got out and let her in. The overhead light came on, but it was off again in a couple of seconds. "What were they doing?"

"Just talking, I think," she said. "I stayed close to the buildings. I don't think they even looked at me, but I don't know for sure. They were too far away to make out."

Lucas shifted into reverse and let the car idle back toward the end of the alley we'd entered. "You did good, kid."

"I got it on the first try," she told me. "The whole $500!"

"Way to go," I said, which sounded lame, but she sounded so goddamn happy about it I had to give her *something*.

"You want the card back?" she asked Lucas.

He glanced out the windshield and then turned his eyes through the back glass again. "Hold on to it," he told her. "We're gonna do it again once we get over the state line."

There were no cars on the street. We eased out, he put it in drive, and we were gone.

83

Dave

Sitting the backseat of Lucas' Batmobile was like being stuffed in a goddamn matchbox and left to die. Usually it wasn't so bad, but I don't think I'd ever ridden back there with anybody else, or for more than like an hour at a time. Not to mention the fact that after spending the last two days getting my ass kicked, sucking in cleanser fumes, doing a lot of grunt work and taking a nice little open-boat ride on a chilly autumn night, I could already feel a nasty cold settling into my bones. My sinuses were burning like I'd spent the whole day in a pool with a bad chlorine mix and snot was starting to trickle down the back of my throat, which felt like I'd been drinking ground-glass milkshakes.

All I wanted to do at that point was down a bottle of cherry Ny-Quil, curl up under a blanket and wait to pass out. Lucas had other plans. He usually does. And most of the time, they don't involve stopping to lie down.

I was almost out of it when he stopped the car again in the middle of nowhere and killed the engine. He got out and took the keys with him, a couple of seconds later I heard the trunk pop. "Is he getting rid of that stuff?" I managed to mumble.

"Yeah," Rachel said. "We're on some kind of bridge. Are you okay? You sound terrible."

"If we don't stop and get some medicine and some Kleenex pretty soon, I'm gonna start blowing snot on the closest thing to my face. Which at this point is either my knees or this chick's hair."

"Yuck," Vampira said, and tried to move away from me. I would have wished her luck, if I'd had the energy. There was no way two people could sit back there without touching each other somehow.

Lucas shut the trunk and got back in, handing me a can of Mountain Dew and what was left of a fifth of cheap vodka we'd packed before we torched the house. "Drink up," he said. "It's good for what ails you."

Unless he'd heard me snorting my own snot back there, I don't know how he knew that anything was ailing me in the first place. I'd tried to be discreet about it, but there's no fooling that guy.

The first swig of vodka burned and almost came out my nose, but I got it down. The second and third slid in easy, and the Mountain Dew washed the taste out of my mouth. I didn't know if it was going to cure anything, but at least I'd be able to get drunk enough not to give a shit.

"I don't want to be a pain in the ass or anything?" Vampira said. "But I'm really, really hungry."

Lucas started the car and we moved. "Hang in there, kid. I've got something for you, but we gotta do a little more banking first."

We rode around through some more empty fields in the dark and came into Burlington from some weird angle. Lucas drove around until he found an all-night Wal-Mart and let Vampira out of the car again. "Cash machine, same deal," he told her. "I don't know how much you can get, but give it a shot."

"Won't they be suspicious?" she said. "I mean, you know, it's like, after curfew and stuff."

"Anybody asks, tell them you're with your dad," he said. "I doubt anybody will."

She was gone awhile, I don't know how long. Lucas and Mrs. Lucas were talking about something or other in the front seat, I don't know what. I know that Mrs. Lucas was starting to get antsy before the chick came back. And she was carrying a sack, which wasn't part of the deal.

Lucas let her in. "I got stuff," she said. "That's okay, isn't it? I mean, we needed stuff."

She pulled a box of Hostess Cupcakes and a toothbrush

out of the bag and handed the rest of it to me. She'd gone all out, too--there was a box of Day-Quil tablets, a bottle of cherry Ny-Quil, a box of Kleenex, a bag of cherry cough drops, a bottle of Advil, and a bottle of orange Gatorade.

"Holy crap," I said. "Thanks."

She handed Lucas the rest of the money. "I couldn't get as much this time," she said. "I only got like $200, minus what I spent."

Lucas flipped through the bills, nodded, and stuffed them into the pocket of his jeans. "That's okay."

"You want the card back now?"

I could see Lucas' eyes in the rearview, but there was nothing in them. "Nah, hold on to it," he said. "I'm making you treasurer. You can hack that, right?"

"Sure," she said.

We stopped at a gas station, and Mrs. Lucas bought cigarettes, cold bottles of Mountain Dew for her and Lucas, and a carton of white milk for Vampira, who asked for it specifically. It seemed a little weird, but I guess if I was gonna wolf down a bunch of chocolate cupcakes, I'd want some milk to go with it too. I don't know if I'd drink gas station milk, but hey, to each his own.

I took two Day-Quil and four Advil and washed them down with the rest of my Mountain Dew so I could use the can for an ashtray. The Ny-Quil was tempting, but I held off on it. I had the feeling we weren't done for the night, and I didn't want to be groggy for whatever came next.

We weren't that far out of town when Lucas opened the middle console and took out a sandwich baggie full of something. "Hey Gretchen," he said. "You've done drugs before, right?"

She swallowed a mouthful of cupcake and leaned forward. "Drugs? Uh, yeah. Some, I mean."

"Ever eat mushrooms?"

"No," she said. "I mostly get high and do some coke, if somebody's got some. I did acid a couple of times."

He stuck his arm into the backseat, the baggie swinging like a pendulum. "You want some?"

She stared at them. "Sure," she said, and took the bag from his hand. "How many should I eat?"

"Try half of them," Lucas said. "That should be enough, for your first time. They don't taste so good. They'll probably make you want to throw up, but try to keep them down. You can eat them with a cupcake, that'll make them go down easier."

"Cool," she said. She peeled the top of the baggie apart and plucked one out. It didn't look like anything I'd want to put in my mouth, but then again, that chick had probably had a lot of things in her mouth that I wouldn't touch. She popped it in and chewed it with a grimace, but she didn't say anything. Thank God. I was sick of talking.

84

Rachel

The park was one of those sad little roadside deals, a couple of ragged ball diamonds, some rusting and sun-bleached playground equipment, and a few oversized wooden picnic tables with layers of green paint slapped over years of pocketknife graffiti. There were a couple of small pavilions--just tin roofs and the poles that held them up-- one built by the local Lions Club and one by the Kiwanis. They had permanent brick grills built into the ends of them, the steel grates removed and locked away for the year. Low piles of dead leaves lay at their bases, waiting for a broom or an off-direction gust of wind to clean them away.

It seemed a little early to be stretching our legs, but when Lucas said that was what he wanted to do, we were all for it. The park was deserted--it was too late, too cold, and too far out of town. There was a pale orange glow to the east of us where the streetlights topped out on the cloud cover, but we couldn't actually see the lights themselves. I don't know what the name of the town was. I don't remember ever seeing a sign, although I'm sure there was one. I was too busy watching Gretchen.

The mushrooms Lucas had given her didn't take long to kick in, and when they did, you could tell. She was staring out the windows, at her hands, at the lights in the dashboard. Every time another vehicle passed us on the highway, I could see that her pupils were huge. Amazed chuckles came out of her every few minutes and ended almost as soon as they began when something else caught her attention. I sort of missed the whole fascination-with-drugs phase that a lot of people go through, so I had no idea what was happening inside her head, but she seemed to be enjoying it.

Lucas guided her to a picnic table beyond the pavilions, close to the pine trees that made up the back border of the park, and took a seat on top of it beside her. "How you doing there, kid?" he said.

"I'm *awesome*," she said. "I feel really, really good. I can't believe I never did this before. It's like I totally missed out on something good and pure and true, you know? It's kind of making me sad to think about it, but I don't want to think about it, cause I don't want to be sad."

"No," he said.

She was rubbing her palms on her thighs, a murmur of pleasure escaping her throat. "Yeah, yeah. Totally. Right. *Totally right,* I mean. I wish these fucking clouds weren't here so I could see the stars. I bet the stars are *beautiful* when you're like this, aren't they? I bet they're everything you always wished stars would be when you looked at them. And snow! That's gotta be the best! You think it might snow tonight, before this wears off, I mean?"

"I doubt it," Lucas shrugged. He lit a cigarette. "It's a little early."

"Oh," she said, and for a moment she was completely crestfallen. But she snapped back with her next breath. "Can I take these again the next time it snows? That would be so bad-ass!"

Lucas watched the end of his cigarette glow in the dark and didn't answer. It was the first time I noticed he had a pair of black gloves on.

Dave had found a seat on a nearby swing and was rocking back and forth, the fifth of vodka in his hand. The rusty chains were creaking as he moved, his feet planted in the hard-packed rut underneath him, his eyes fixed on some distant spot in the general direction of the highway. I didn't know how much he was planning on drinking, but the idea of being wasted and sick in the back of the Camaro didn't seem too appealing.

When I looked back at Gretchen, she was crying. Big, thick tears that rolled down her cheeks and framed her mouth, leaving snail-trails of shine before falling off her chin and disappearing. "I can't believe I did that," she said in quiet sobs. "I *killed* him. He was another person, a human being, and I *killed* him. *Why did I* do *that?* I knew it wasn't gonna feel good. It didn't make me feel any better at all. *And he's still dead and I can't take it back.*"

A burst of wind hissed against the pines. "What about what he did to you?" Lucas said. "Could he take that back? You think he wanted to?"

"No," she choked out, and buried her face in her hands. "But that doesn't make it good."

I was glad I wasn't close enough to put an arm around her. I would have done it. And since I knew what was coming, it wouldn't have helped anybody, then or later.

"I want to be good," she said. "I want to be *happy*. I never get to be happy, ever. Other people get to be happy. They get to have friends and people who love them and good times. Why not me? How come I'm always the bad one, the fucked-up one? What did I *do*? If somebody would just tell me maybe I could fix it, or I could be different and people would forget. I could run away forever and go somewhere nobody knows me and not do anything bad again and be somebody else and people would like me. *I would like me.* I just need somebody to tell me. I'm not even old enough to drive and everything is already so bad. I'm already so *worthless.* How can life be like that? I never even got to do anything good and I'm already fucked forever."

Lucas pinched out the end of his cigarette and stuck it in the pocket of his hoodie. "You believe in God?" he asked her. "You religious at all?"

"I don't know," she sniffed. "What, like church and all that? We used to all go, when I was a little kid, but then I wouldn't go anymore. All those people were always staring at me in there, like they were better than me, like they knew everything about me and I wasn't good enough to be there. I don't know if I believe in God. I don't think about him anymore, cause I'm pretty sure he hasn't thought about me in like, *forever.* I used to pray sometimes, even after I quit going to church and everything, but it never worked. Nothing ever got any better. I haven't done it for a long time. It makes me feel like a fucking idiot."

Her head snapped around, like a snake going for a mouse. "Why, do you believe in him? Are you religious?"

One side of Lucas' mouth went back. "Me? Nah. He might be up there somewhere, but he lost my vote a long time ago. I've read the books, though. I know how he's supposed to work, if he does."

"Do you pray?" Gretchen said. "Do you ask Him for stuff when you're in trouble?"

Lucas shook his head. "I gave up on that when I was younger than you. But you know what I think?"

Gretchen giggled and swiped at a clear runner of snot that was creeping down her lip. "What?"

"If he's up there, or out there, or wherever, then he's probably pretty good. I don't think he ever makes anybody's life worse than it would have been otherwise. He's just awful fucking particular about who he decides to stick up for. He's got hard rules, he's a total bastard, but he's good. And I think if you believe in him, when it's time, when you're completely up against it and there's nothing left for you, he'll help you out."

"Oh *man*," she giggled. "That's messed up. You really believe that?"

"More or less," Lucas nodded. "That's the short version of it, anyway." He plucked at a stray lock of hair that had gotten tangled in his goatee and tucked it back behind his ear. "You believe in heaven, right?"

"Yeah," she said. "I guess so. Not that it matters. I ain't never gonna get there."

"Anybody can get into heaven," he told her. "Anybody. Doesn't matter what you did or what you wanted to do, you can still get in. There's a loophole."

I moved closer to them. I wasn't sure what he was working on, but I didn't want to miss a word of it. When I glanced over at Dave I saw that he was looking at us. I couldn't hear it, but it looked like he was laughing.

"God doesn't have loopholes," Gretchen snickered. "Does he? I mean, He's *God*. He thinks of everything.

That's the whole point."

"There is no point," Lucas told her. "He's God. If he's there. We're us, and we're here. And it's a long way between us and him."

She mulled this over. It was strange to watch her, tears still rolling down her cheeks at a steady pace even though she didn't seem to be upset anymore. This total feeling of isolation hit me, broke over me like a wave and soaked me to the bone. Outside, in the dark, in the cold, waiting for something I knew was going to happen but not exactly how. Knowing that it was going to be bad. That it was going to be final. And Dave off to my left, swaying back and forth on rusty chains with his bottle of vodka, laughing and sick. Everything was fast and out of control, from the sky to the ground and in every direction, and I was in the middle of it.

"You've had it bad. And you're always going to have it bad, as long as you live," Lucas said.

"Ah, don't say that," she sighed.

"You can get away from everything but yourself," Lucas said. "And you're what's killing you. It's not your fault. The damage has been done. It's never going to get any better."

"Ah fuck," she said. There was no venom in it. "Don't say that, man. Don't tell me that."

"It's the truth. I gave you those shrooms to open you up because I like you. I really do. I think you could have been good, before they got to you. It's too late now. You've been defiled. But I wanted you to see just one time how beautiful life can be."

"You're gonna kill me," she sobbed. "Aren't you? Don't do that. Please."

"This is the loophole," Lucas said, and slipped an arm around her back to brace her. "God wants you to repent, to beg for forgiveness for all the things you had to do while he ignored you, all the times you were weak and took the easy way out in his eyes. But if you don't do it right, he'll toss you aside like a bag of trash and let you burn."

"No," she moaned. "Please, no."

"They're his rules, not mine," Lucas said. "And we're gonna cheat him. I'm gonna cheat him for you, because you deserve better. If you die quick, so quick you don't have time to beg for his forgiveness, he lets you in. If you can't do it, then you can't do it wrong."

I thought he was going to hug her when his arm came up. She did too--there's no other explanation for why she turned to him then, her own arms ready to wrap around his shoulders, her chin up as if in preparation for a kiss she was about to receive.

The blade of the buck-knife made no sound at all as it slid around her throat and spilled her heat into the chilled, damp air with a pathetic wisp of steam that was gone almost before it appeared.

She gasped and lurched forward as if to fall on him, but his hand on her back held her away. The first spurt of blood missed him by a fraction. The second dropped on her lap and the bench of the picnic table between her Doc Martens with a sound like somebody vomiting. The third was weak and landed on the front of the baby blue zip-up sweatshirt

I'd lent her. Staining it forever.

Lucas eased her back from the waist, laid her flat on the table while the heels of her boots drummed an irregular beat on the weather-scarred bench. Her hands twitched, rose and fell, grasped for something, anything, and came up short. In a few seconds she was still. It was over.

He stared into her eyes as they went glassy. There was no expression on his face that I could make out; it was too dark to get a good look at his eyes. For those few moments he was one statue posed over another. Take away the clothes and carve them out of marble, substitute a pedestal for the picnic table, and they could have been a classic work of art, a monument on a Greek isle. The kind that inspires awe, that demands you create a story in your head to give the whole thing a perspective you can live with.

He wiped the blade of the knife on her black jean-clad thigh and folded it into his own pocket, stepping down off the table with a long, fluid stride that made the change jingle in his pockets. "Let's go."

Dave was still in his swing. He'd stopped moving. His right temple was pressed against one of the rusty chains that held him up, the bottle of vodka in his left hand, between his knees, with a couple of inches left in it. I couldn't tell if he was sick or drunk. When he saw we were on the move he vaulted himself up, hanging on the chain to steady himself for a second before his balance kicked in and he shambled after us, grinning.

"I feel like shit," he said as I held the passenger seat up for him so he could climb into the back. "It's fucking awesome."

The motor fired up on the first turn of the key. Lucas didn't pull the knob for the headlights until we were on the highway, the park a misty blob of light in our mirrors, no sign of traffic in either direction. When he saw me shivering he turned on the heater, the first gust of hot air that came out of the vents laced with the smell of a garage I'd never been in. As my body warmed up I settled back beneath the seatbelt, staring out the window and edging toward sleep, empty but content.

I wanted to know everything about him. I wanted to know his whole life story, from the first thing he ever remembered right up to that moment. Every single detail. And it was the best kind of wanting.

I knew it would never be answered.

There was no way that it could ever disappoint.

To Be Continued in:

The Lost Art of Keeping a Secret

Kevin Mellor lives in central Illinois and is a graduate of Western Illinois University. *The Gentle Art of Making Enemies* is his first published novel.

www.kevinmellor.com